Black Classics

strong women and strutting men

Published by *Black Classics*
An imprint of The X Press
6 Hoxton Square, London N1 6NU
Tel: 0171 729 1199
Fax: 0171 729 1771

Printed by LEGO of Italy

Distributed in US by INBOOK, 1436 West Randolph Street, Chicago, Illinois 60607, USA Orders 1-800 626 4330 Fax orders 1-800 334 3892

Distributed in UK by Turnaround Distribution, Unit 3, Olympia Trading Estate, Coburg Road, London N22 6TZ
Tel: 0181 829 3000
Fax: 0181 881 5088

ISBN 1-874509-81-6

Introduction

The black woman as novelist is a powerful and exciting force in contemporary fiction, for she is the prism through which the searing rays or race, class and sex are first focused and then refracted. You may paint her in poetry or fiction as a frail vine, clinging to her brotherman for support and dying when deprived of it, and all this may sound well enough to please the imaginations of lovelorn schoolgirls. But the black woman - the true black woman wants more. She is a student. A graduate. A wife. A professional. A divorcee. A mother. A lover. A child of the ghetto and a product of the bourgeoisie. A warrior. A person who never dreamed she would write books. A peacemaker. A solitary individual. A conscious woman. A gentle humanist. A violent revolutionary. The black woman is: Angry and tender. Loving and hating. All these things and more.

Strong Women and Strutting Men is a unique collection of fiction by black women, stretching a diverse range of the emotions and experiences of black women through time. Share with me the pleasure in reading these classic authors of black literature:

Marcia Williams
London, September 1999

BRO' ABR'M JIMSON'S WEDDING
Pauline E. Hopkins

It was a Sunday in early spring the first time that Caramel Johnson dawned on the congregation of this church in a populous New England city.

The Afro-Americans of that city are well-to-do, being of a frugal nature, and considering it a lasting disgrace for any man among them, desirous of social standing in the community, not to make himself comfortable in this world's goods against the coming time, when old age creeps on apace and renders him unfit for active business.

Therefore the members of the said church had not waited to be exhorted by reformers to own their unpretentious homes and small farms outside the city limits, but they vied with each other in efforts to accumulate a small competency urged thereto by a realisation of what pressing needs the future might

1

bring, or it might have been because of the constant
example of white neighbors, and a due respect for the
dignity which their foresight had brought to the
'superior' race.

Of course, these small Vanderbilts and Astors of a
darker hue must have a place of worship in accord with
their worldly prosperity, and so it was that this church
was the richest plum in the ecclesiastical pudding, and
greatly sought by scholarly divines as a resting place for
four years — the extent of the time-limit allowed by
conference to the men who must be provided with
suitable charges according to the demands of their
energy and scholarship.

The attendance was unusually large for morning
service, and a restless movement was noticeable all
through the sermon. How strange a thing is nature; the
change of the seasons announces itself in all humanity
as well as in the trees and flowers, the grass, and in the
atmosphere. Something within us responds instantly to
the touch of kinship that dwells in all life.

The air, soft and balmy, laden with rich promise for
the future, came through the massive, half-open
windows, blowing in refreshing waves upon the
congregation. The sunlight fell through the colored
glass of the windows in prismatic hues, and dancing all
over the lofty star-gemmed ceiling, painted the hue of
the broad vault of heaven, creeping down in crinkling
shadows to touch the deep garnet cushions of the sacred
desk, and the rich wood of the altar with a hint of gold.

The offertory was ended. The silvery cadences of a

rich soprano voice still lingered in the air:

Oh, Worship the Lord in the beauty of holiness.

There was a suppressed feeling of expectation, but not the faintest rustle as the minister rose in the pulpit, and after a solemn pause, gave the usual invitation:

"If there is anyone in this congregation desiring to unite with this church, either by letter or on probation, please come forward to the altar."

The words had not died upon his lips when a woman started from her seat near the door and passed up the main aisle. There was a sudden commotion on all sides. Many heads were turned — it takes so little to interest a church audience. The girls in the choir-box leaned over the rail, nudged each other and giggled, while the men said to one another, "She's a stunner, and no mistake."

The candidate for membership, meanwhile, had reached the altar railing and stood before the man of God, to whom she had handed her letter from a former Sabbath home, with head decorously bowed as became the time and the holy place. There was no denying the fact that she was a pretty girl; brown of skin, small of feature, with an ever-lurking gleam of laughter in eyes coal black. Her figure was slender and beautifully moulded, with a seductive grace in the undulating walk and erect carriage. But the chief charm of the sparkling dark face lay in its intelligence, and the responsive play of facial expression which was enhanced by two mischievous dimples pressed into the rounded cheeks by the caressing fingers of the god of Love.

The minister whispered to the candidate, coughed, blew his nose on his snowy clerical handkerchief and, finally, turned to the expectant congregation:

"Sister Chocolate Caramel Johnson—"

He was interrupted by a snicker and a suppressed laugh, again from the choir-box, and an audible whisper which sounded distinctly throughout the quiet church.

"I'd get the Legislature to change that if it was mine, 'deed I would."

Then silence profound caused by the reverend's stern glance of reproval bent on the offenders in the choir-box.

"Such levity will not be allowed among the members of the choir. If it occurs again, I shall ask the choir master for the names of the offenders and have their places taken by those more worthy to be gospel singers."

Thereupon Mrs. Tilly Anderson whispered to Mrs. Nancy Tobias that, "Them choir gals is the most deceiving hussies in the church, and for my part, I'm glad the pastor called 'em down That sister's too good looking for 'em, and they'll be after her like a pack of hounds, mind me, Sis Tobias."

Sister Tobias ducked her head in her lap and shook her fat sides in laughing appreciation of the sister's foresight.

Order being restored the minister proceeded:

"Sister Chocolate Caramel Johnson brings a letter to us from our sister church in Nashville, Tennessee. She has been a member in good standing for ten years, having been received into fellowship at ten years of age. She leaves them now, much to their regret, to pursue the study of music at one of the large conservatories in this city, and they recommend her to our love and care. You know the contents of the letter. All in favor of giving Sister Johnson the right hand of fellowship, please manifest the same by a rising vote."

The whole congregation rose.

"Contrary minded? None. The ayes have it. Be seated, friends. Sister Johnson, it gives me great pleasure to receive you into this church. I welcome you to its joys and sorrows. May God bless you, Brother Jimson?" Brother Jimson stepped from his seat to the pastor's side. "I assign this sister to your class. Sister Johnson, this is Brother Jimson, your future spiritual teacher."

Brother Jimson shook the hand of his new member, warmly, and she returned to her seat. The minister pronounced the benediction over the waiting congregation; the organ burst into richest melody. Slowly the crowd of worshippers dispersed.

Abraham Jimson had made his money as a janitor for the wealthy people of the city. He was a bachelor, and when reproved by some good Christian brother for still dwelling in single blessedness, always offered as an excuse that he had been too busy to think of a wife, but that now he was well fixed pecuniarily, he would begin to look over his lady friends for a suitable companion.

He owned a house in the suburbs and a fine brick

dwelling in the city proper. He was a trustee of prominence in the church; in fact, its 'solid man', and his opinion was sought and his advice acted upon by his associates on the Board. It was felt that any lady in the congregation would be proud to know herself his choice.

When Caramel Johnson received the right hand of fellowship, her aunt, the widow Maria Nash, was ahead in the race for the wealthy class-leader. It had been neck-and-neck for a while between her and Sister Viney Peters, but finally it had settled down to Sister Maria with a hundred to one, among the sporting members of the Board, that she carried off the prize, for Sister Maria owned a house adjoining Brother Jimson's in the suburbs, and property counts these days.

Sister Nash had no idea when she sent for her niece to come that the latter would prove a rival; her son Andy was as good as engaged to Caramel. But it is always the unexpected that happens. Caramel came, and Brother Jimson had no eyes for the charms of other women after he had gazed into her coal black orbs, and watched her dimples come and go.

Caramel decided to accept a position as housemaid in order to help defray the expenses of her tuition at the conservatory, and Brother Jimson interested himself so warmly in her behalf that she soon had a situation in the home of his richest patron where it was handy for him to chat with her about the business of the church, and the welfare of her soul, in general. Things progressed very smoothly until the fall, when one day Sister Maria had occasion to call unexpectedly on her niece, and found Brother Jimson basking in her smiles while he enjoyed a sumptuous dinner of roast chicken.

To say that Sister Maria was set way back would not accurately describe her feelings; but from that time Abraham Jimson knew that he had a secret foe in the Widow Nash.

Before many weeks had passed it was publicly known that Brother Jimson would lead Caramel Johnson to the altar come Christmas." There was much sly speculation as to the widow's getting left, and how she took it from those who had cast hopeless glances toward the chief man of the church. Great preparations were set for the wedding festivities. The bride's trousseau was a present from the groom and included a white satin wedding gown and a costly gold watch. The town house was refurnished, and a trip to New York was in contemplation.

"Hump," grunted Sister Nash when told the rumors, "there's no fool like an ole fool. Car'mel's a handful he'll find, if he gits her."

"I reckon he'll get her all right, Sis Nash," laughed the neighbor, who had run in to talk over the news.

"I've said my word and I ain't going change it, Sis. Mind me. I says, if he gits her, and I mean it."

Andy Nash was also a member of Brother Jimson's class; he possessed, too, a strong sweet baritone voice which made him of great value to the choir. He was an immense success in the social life of the city, and had created sad havoc with the hearts of the colored girls.

He could have his pick of the best of them because of his graceful figure and fine easy manners. Until Caramel had been dazzled by the wealth of her elderly lover, she had considered herself fortunate as the lady of his choice.

It was Sunday, three weeks before the wedding that Andy resolved to have it out with Caramel.

"She's been hot and she's been cold, and now she's luke warm, and today ends it before this gentleman sleeps," he told himself as he stood before the mirror and tied his pale blue silk tie in a stunning knot.

Brother Jimson's class was a popular one and had a large membership; the hour spent there was much enjoyed, even by visitors. Andy went into the vestry early, resolved to meet Caramel if possible. She was there, at the back of the room sitting alone on a settee. Andy immediately seated himself in the vacant place by her side. There were whispers and much head-shaking among the few early worshippers, all of whom knew the story of the young fellow's romance and his disappointment.

As he dropped into the seat beside her, Caramel turned her large eyes on him intently, speculatively, with a doubtful sort of curiosity suggested in her expression, as to how he took her flagrant desertion.

"Howdy, Car'mel?" was his greeting without a shade of resentment.

"I'm well; no need to ask how you are," was the quick response. There was a mixture of cordiality and coquetry in her manner. Her eyes narrowed and glittered under lowered lids, as she gave him a long side-glance. How could she help showing her admiration for the supple young giant beside her? 'Surely', she told herself, 'I'll have long time enough to get sick of old rheumatics', her pet name for her elderly lover.

"I ain't sick much," was Andy's surly reply.

He leaned his elbow on the back of the settee and gave his recent sweetheart a flaming glance of mingled love and hate, oblivious to the presence of the assembled class members.

"You ain't over friendly these days, Car'mel, but I gits news of your capers round 'bout some of the members."

"Yes?" she answered as she flashed her great eyes at him in pretended surprise. He laughed a laugh not good to hear.

"Yes," he drawled. Then he added with sudden energy "Are you going to tie up to old Rheumatism sure 'nuff, come Christmas?"

"Come Christmas, Andy, I be. I hate to tell you, but I have to do it."

He recoiled as from a blow. As for the girl, she found a keen relish in the situation; it flattered her vanity.

"How comes you've changed your mind, Car'mel, 'bout you and me? You've told me often that I was your first choice."

"Well," she drawled, glancing uneasily about her and avoiding her aunt's gaze, which she knew was bent upon her every movement, "I did reckon once I would.

But a man with money suits me best, and you ain't got a cent."

"No more have you. You ain't no better than other women to work and help a man along, is you?"

The color flamed an instant in her face turning the dusky skin to a deep, dull red.

"Andy Nash, you always was a fool, and as ignorant as a wild Injun. I mean to have a sure nuff brick house and plenty of money. That makes people respect you. Why don't you quit being so shiftless and save your money. You ain't worth your salt."

"Your head's turned with piano-playing and living up North. If you'll turn him off and come back home, I'll turn over a new leaf, Car'mel," his voice was soft and persuasive enough now.

She had risen to her feet; her eyes flashed, her face was full of pride.

"I won't. I've quit liking you, Andy Nash."

"Are you in earnest?" he asked, also rising from his seat.

"Dead earnest."

"Then there's no more to be said."

He spoke calmly, not raising his voice above a whisper. She stared at him in surprise. Then he added as he swung on his heel preparatory to leaving her:

"You ain't got him yet, my gal. But remember, I'm waiting for you when you need me."

While this whispered conference was taking place in the back part of the vestry, Brother Jimson had entered, and many an anxious glance he cast in the direction of the couple. Andy made his way slowly to his mother's side as Brother Jimson rose in his place to open the meeting. There was a commotion on all sides as the members rustled down on their knees for prayer. Widow Nash whispered to her son as they knelt side by side:

"How did you make out, Andy?"

"Didn't make out at all, mammy; she's as obstinate as a mule."

"Well, then, there's only one thing more to do."

Andy was unpleasant company for the remainder of the day. He sought, but found nothing to palliate Caramel's treachery. He had only surly, bitter words for his companions who ventured to address him, as the outward expression of inward tumult. The more he brooded over his wrongs the worse he felt. When he went to work on Monday morning he was feeling vicious. He had made up his mind to do something desperate. The wedding should not come off. He would be avenged.

Andy went about his work at the hotel in gloomy silence unlike his usual gay hilarity. It happened that all the female help at the great hostelry was white, and on that particular Monday morning it was the duty of Bridget McCarthy's watch to clean the floors. Bridget was also not in the best of humors, for Pat McClosky, her special company, had gone to the priest's with her rival, Kate Connerton, on Sunday afternoon, and Bridget had not yet got over the effects of a strong rum punch taken to quiet her nerves after hearing the news.

Bridget had scrubbed a wide swath of the marble floor when Andy came through with a rush order carried in scientific style high above his head, balanced on one hand.

Intent upon satisfying the guest who was princely in his tips, Andy's unwary feet became entangled in the maelstrom of brooms, scrubbing-brushes and pails. In an instant the order was sliding over the floor in a general mix-up.

To say Bridget was mad wouldn't do her state justice. She forgot herself and her surroundings and relieved her feelings in elegant Irish, ending a tirade of abuse by calling Andy a wall-eyed, bandy-legged nigger.

Andy couldn't stand that from common, poor white trash, so calling all his science into play he struck out straight from the shoulder with his right, and delivered a swinging blow on the mouth, which seated her neatly in the five-gallon bowl of freshly made lobster salad which happened to be standing on the floor behind her.

There was a wail from the kitchen that reached to every department. It being the busiest hour of the day when they served dinner, the dish-washers and scrubbers went on a strike against the "nigger who struck Bridget McCarthy," mingled with cries of "Lynch him!" Instantly the great basement floor was a battleground. Every colored man seized whatever was handiest and ranged himself by Andy's side, and stood ready to receive the onslaught of the Irish brigade. For the sake of peace, and sorely against his inclinations, the proprietor surrendered Andy to the police on a charge of assault and battery.

On Wednesday morning of that eventful week, Brother Jimson made his way to his house in the suburbs to collect the rent. Unseen by the eye of man, he was wrestling with a problem that had shadowed his life for many years. No one on earth suspected him unless it might be the widow. Brother Jimson boasted of his consistent Christian life, rolled his piety like a sweet morsel beneath his tongue, and had deluded himself into thinking that he could do no sin. There were scoffers in the church who doubted the genuineness of his pretensions, and he believed that there was a movement against his power led by Widow Nash.

Brother Jimson groaned in bitterness of spirit. His only fear was that he might be parted from Caramel. If he lost her he felt that all happiness in life was over for him, and anxiety gave him a sickening feeling of unrest. He was tormented, too, by jealousy; and when he was called upon by Andy's anxious mother to rescue her son from the clutches of the law, he had promised her fair enough, but in reality resolved to do nothing but tell the judge that Andy was a dangerous character whom it was best to quell by severity. The pastor and all the other influential members of the church were at court on Tuesday, but Brother Jimson was conspicuous by his absence.

Today Brother Jimson resolved to call on Sister Nash, and, as he had heard nothing of the outcome of the trial, made cautious inquiries concerning that, and also sound her on the subject nearest his heart.

He opened the gate and walked down the side path to the back door. From within came the rhythmic sound of a rubbing board. The brother knocked, and then cleared his throat with a preliminary cough.

"Come," called a voice within. As the door swung open it revealed the spare form of the widow, who with sleeves rolled above her elbows stood at the tub cutting her way through piles of foaming suds.

"Morning, Sis Nash. How's all?"

"That you, Bro' Jimson? How's yourself? Take a chair and make yourself at home."

"Certainly, Sis Nash, don't care if I do." The good brother scanned the sister with an eagle eye. "Yes, I'm pretty tolerable these days, thank God. Obliged to you, Sister, I just will stop and rest myself before I repair myself back to the city."

He seated himself in the most comfortable chair in the room, tilted it on the two back legs against the wall, lit his pipe and with a grunt of satisfaction settled back to watch the white rings of smoke curl about his head.

"These are mighty ticklish times, Sister. How will you continue on the journey? Is you strong in the faith?"

"I've got the faith, my brother, but I ain't on no mountain top this week. I'm way down in the valley; I'm just coaxing the Lord to keep me sweet," and Sister Nash wiped the suds from her hands and prodded the clothes in the boiler with the clothes-stick, added fresh pieces and went on with her work.

"This is a world strewed with wrecks and floating with tears. It's the valley of tribulation. May your faith continue. I hear Jim Jinkins has bought a farm up Taunton way."

"No!"

"Doctor tells me Bro' Waters is coming after Christmas. They do say as how he's stirring up things terrible; he's easing his mind on this lynching business, and it's high time. High time."

"Sho! Don't say so! What you reckon he's going to tell us now, Brother Jimson?"

"Something astonishing, Sister; it'll stir the country from end to end. Yes, the Council is powerful strong as an organization."

"Sho! Sho!"

And the 'thrub-thrub' of the board could be heard a mile away.

The conversation flagged. Evidently Widow Nash was not in a talkative mood this morning. The brother was disappointed.

"Well, it's mighty comfortable here, but I must be going."

"What's your hurry, Brother Jimson?"

"Business, Sister, business," and the brother brought his chair forward preparatory to rising. "Where's Andy? How'd he come out of that little difficulty?"

"Locked up."

"You don't mean to say he's still in jail?"

"Yes; he's in jail 'til I gits his bail."

"What might the sentence be, Sister?"

"Twenty dollars fine or six months at the Island."

There was silence for a moment, broken only by the

'thrub-thrub' of the washboard, while the smoke curled upward from Brother Jimson's pipe as he enjoyed a few last puffs.

"These are mighty ticklish times, Sister. Poor Andy, the way of the transgressor is hard."

Sister Nash took her hands out of the tub and stood with arms akimbo, a statue of Justice carved in ebony. Her voice was like the trump of doom.

"Yes; and men like you is the cause of it. You leading men with money and chances don't do your duty. I asked you, I asked you fair, to go down to the judge and bail that poor chile out. Did you go? No, you hard-faced old devil, you left him be there, and I had to get the money from my white folks. Yes, and I'm breaking my back now, over that pile of clothes to pay that twenty dollars. Uhm! All the trouble comes to us women."

"That's so, Sister; that's the living truth," murmured Brother Jimson furtively watching the rising storm and wondering where the lightning of her speech would strike next.

"I tell you what, it is our deceitfulness to each other is the reason we don't prosper and God's a-punishing us with fire 'cause we're so jealous and snaky to each other."

"That's so, Sister; that's the living truth."

"Yes, sir; a nigger's bound to be a nigger 'til the trumpet of doom. You can skin him, but he's a nigger still. Broadcloth, boiled shirts and money won't make him more or less, no, suh."

"That's so, Sister; that's just so."

"A nigger can't help himself. White folks can run against the law all the time and they never gits caught, but a nigger! Every time he opens his mouth he puts his foot in it. He had to hit that poor white trash gal in the mouth and get jailed, and leave his poor ole mother to work her fingers to the second joint to get him out. Uhm!"

"These are mighty ticklish times, Sister. Man's bound to sin; it's his natural state. I hope this will teach Andy humility of the spirit."

"A little humility'd be good for yourself, Abr'm Jimson."

Sister Nash ceased her sobs and set her teeth hard.

"Lord, Sister Nash, what comparison is there 'twixt me and a worthless nigger like Andy? My business is with the salt of the earth, and so I have dwelt ever since I was consecrated."

"Salt of the earth. But if the salt has lost its saver how you going salt it again? No, suh, you cain't do it; it must be cast out and trodden underfoot of men. That's what's going to happen you Abe Jimson, here me? And I'd like to trod on you with my foot, and every ole good for nothing bag of salt like you," shouted Sister Nash. "You're a snake in the grass; you done stole the boy's gal and then try to get him sent to the Island. You cain't deny it, for the judge done told me all you said, you ole rhinoceros-hided hypocrite. Salt of the earth. You!"

Brother Jimson regretted that Widow Nash had found him out. Slowly, he turned, settling his hat on the back of his head.

"Good morning, Sister Nash. I ain't got no hard feelings against you. I'm too near to the kingdom to let trifles jar me. My bowels of compassion yearns over you, Sister, a pilgrim and a stranger in this unfriendly world."

No answer from Sister Nash. Brother Jimson lingered.

"Good morning, Sister."

Still no answer.

"I hope to see you at the wedding, Sister."

"Keep on hoping; I'll be there. That gal's my own sister's chile. What in time she wants of a rheumatic ole sap-head like you for, beats me. I wouldn't marry you for no money, myself. No, suh. It's my belief that you've done goophered her."

"Yes, Sister; I've heard tell of people refusing before they was asked," he retorted, giving her a sly look.

For answer the widow grabbed the clothes-stick and flung it at him in speechless rage.

"My, what a temper you've got," remarked Brother Jimson soothingly as he dodged the shovel, the broom and the stove-covers. But he sighed with relief as he turned into the street and caught the faint sound of the washboard now resumed.

To a New Englander, the season of snow and ice with its clear biting atmosphere, is the ideal time for the great festival. Christmas morning dawned in royal splendor; the sun kissed the snowy streets and turned the icicles into brilliant stalactites. The bells rang a joyous call from every steeple, and soon the churches were crowded with eager worshippers eager to hear again the oft-repeated wonderful story on which the heart of the whole Christian world feeds its faith and hope. Words of tender faith, marvelous in their simplicity fell from the lips of a world-renowned preacher, and touched the hearts of the listening multitude:

"The winter sunshine is not more bright and clear than the atmosphere of living joy, which stretching back between our eyes and that picture of Bethlehem shows us its beauty in unstained freshness. And as we open once again those chapters of the gospel in which the ever fresh and living picture stands, there seems from year to year always to come some newer, brighter meaning into the words that tell the tale.

"St. Matthew says that when Jesus was born in Bethlehem the wise men came from the East to Jerusalem. The East means man's search after God; Jerusalem means God's search after man. The East means the religion of the devout soul; Jerusalem means the religion of the merciful God. The East means Job's cry, 'Oh, that I knew where I might find him. Jerusalem means 'Immanuel — God with us'."

Then the deep-toned organ joined the grand chorus of human voices in a fervent hymn of praise and thanksgiving:

> Lo! the Morning Star appeareth,
> O'er the world His beams are cast;

> He the Alpha and Omega,
> He, the Great, the First the Last!
> Hallelujah! Hallelujah!
> Let the heavenly portal ring!
> Christ is born, the Prince of glory!
> Christ the Lord, Messiah, King!

Everyone of prominence in church circles had been bidden to the Jimson wedding. The presents were many and costly. Early after service on Christmas morning the vestry room was taken in hand by leading sisters to prepare the tables for the supper, for on account of the host of friends bidden to the feast, the reception was to be held in the vestry.

The tables groaned beneath their loads of turkey, salads, pies, puddings, cakes and fancy ices. Yards and yards of evergreen wreaths encircled the granite pillars, the altar was banked with potted plants and cut flowers. It was a beautiful sight. The main aisle was roped off for the invited guests, with white satin ribbons.

Brother Jimson's patrons were to be present in a body, and they had sent the bride a solid silver service so magnificent that the sisters could only sigh with envy.

The ceremony was to take place at seven sharp. Long before that hour the ushers in full evening dress were ready to receive the guests.

Sister Maria Nash was among the first to arrive, and even the Queen of Sheba was not arrayed like unto her. At fifteen minutes before the hour, the organist began an elaborate instrumental performance. There was an expectant hush and much head-turning when the music changed to the familiar strains of the Wedding March. The minister took his place inside the railing ready to receive the party. The groom waited at the altar.

First came the ushers, then the maids of honor, then the flower girl daughter of a prominent member carrying a basket of flowers which she scattered before the bride, who was on the arm of the best man. In the bustle and confusion at the entrance of the wedding party no one noticed a group of strangers accompanied by Andy Nash, enter and occupy seats near the door.

The service began. All was quiet. The pastor's words fell clearly upon the listening ears. He had reached the words:

"If any man can show just cause..." when like a thunderclap came a voice from the back part of the house — an angry excited voice, and a woman of ponderous avoirdupois advanced up the aisle.

"Hold on there, pastor, hold on. A man cain't have but one wife 'cause it's against the law. I'm Abe Jimson's lawful wife and here are his six children — all boys — to point out their daddy."

In an instant the assembly was in confusion.

"My soul," exclaimed Viney Peters, "the ole serpent. And to think how near I come to taking up with him. I'm glad I ain't Car'mel."

Sis Maria said nothing, but a smile of triumph lit up her countenance.

"Brother Jimson, is this true?" demanded the

minister sternly. But Abraham Jimson was past answering. His face was ashen, his teeth chattering, his hair standing on end. His shaking limbs refused to uphold his weight; he sank upon his knees on the steps of the altar.

But now a hand was laid upon his shoulder and Mrs Jimson hauled him up on his feet with a jerk.

"Abe Jimson, you know me. You ran away from me up North fifteen years ago, and you hid yourself like a ground hog in a hole, but I've got you. There'll be no new wife in the Jimson family this week. I'm your first wife and I'll be your last one. Get up here now, you miserable sinner and tell the pastor who I be."

Brother Jimson meekly obeyed the clarion voice. His sanctified air had vanished, his pride humbled into the dust.

"Pastor," came in trembling tones from his quivering lips. "These are mighty ticklish times." He paused. A deep silence followed his words. "I'm a weak-kneed, miserable sinner. I have fallen under temptation. This is Ma Jane, my wife, and these here boys is my sons. God forgive me."

The bride, who had been forgotten now, broke in:

"Abraham Jimson, you ought to be hung. I'm going to sue you for breach of promise." It was a fatal remark. Mrs. Jimson turned upon her.

"You will, will you? Sue him, will you? I'll make a chocolate Car'mel of you before I'm done with you, you deceitful hussy, hoodooing honest men from their wives."

She sprang upon the girl, tearing, biting, rendering. The satin gown and gossamer veil were reduced to rags. Caramel emitted a series of ear-splitting shrieks, but the biting and tearing went on. How it might have ended no one can tell if Andy had not sprang over the backs of the pews and grappled with the infuriated woman.

The excitement was intense. Men and women struggled to get out of the church. Some jumped from the windows and others crawled under the pews, where they were secure from violence. In the midst of the melee, Brother Jimson disappeared and was never seen again, and Mrs. Jimson came into possession of his property by due process of law.

In the church Abraham Jimson's wedding and his fall from grace is still spoken of in eloquent whispers.

In the home of Mrs. Andy Nash a motto adorns the parlor walls worked in scarlet wool and handsomely framed in gilt. The text reads: *Ye are the salt of the earth; there is nothing hidden that shall not be revealed.*

GENERAL WASHINGTON
Pauline E. Hopkins

General Washington did any odd jobs he could find
around the market, but his specialty was selling chitlins.

He lived in the very shady atmosphere of Murderer's
Bay in the capital city. All that he could remember of
father or mother in his ten years of miserable babyhood
was that they were frequently absent from the little
shanty where they were supposed to live, generally
after a protracted spell of drunkenness and bloody
quarrels when the police were forced to interfere for the
peace of the community. During these absences, the
child would drift from one squalid home to another
wherever a woman — God save the mark — would take
pity upon the poor waif and throw him a few scraps of
food for his starved stomach, or a rag or a shawl, apron
or skirt to wrap about his little body.

One night, the General's daddy being on a short
vacation in the city, came home to supper. As there was

no supper to eat, he occupied himself in beating his wife. After the police officers took him, the General's daddy never returned to his home. The General's mammy? Oh, she died.

General Washington's resources developed rapidly after this. Said resources consisted of a pair of nimble feet for dancing the hoe-down, shuffles intricate and dazzling, and the Juba; a strong pair of lungs, a wardrobe limited to a pair of pants originally made for a man, and tied about the ankles with strings, a shirt, a vast amount of 'brass', and a very, very small amount of nickel.

His education was practical: "If a corn-dodger costs two cents and a fellah ain't got the two cents, how's he going to get the corn-dodger?"

General Washington ranked first among the knights of the pavement. He could shout louder and hit harder than any among them; that was the reason they called him 'General'.

The General could curse, too, I am sorry to admit it, but the truth must be told.

He uttered an oath when he caught a crowd of small white aristocrats tormenting a kitten. The General landed among them in quick time and commenced knocking heads at a lively rate. Presently he was master of the situation, and marched away triumphantly with the kitten in his arms, followed by stones and other missiles which whirled about him through space from behind the safe shelter of backyards and street corners.

The General took the kitten home. Home was a dry-

goods box turned on end and filled with straw for
winter. He was as happy as a lord in summer, but the
winter was a trial. The last winter had been a hard one,
and the General called a meeting of the leading
members of the gang to consider the advisability of
moving farther south for the hard weather.

" 'Pears to me, fellas, Washington's heap colder'n it
used to be, and I'm mighty unscrupulous 'bout staying
here."

"Business is mighty good," said Teenie, the smallest
member of the gang, "s'pose we put off moving 'til after
Christmas? Jeemes Henry, fellas, it ain't no Christmas
for me outside of Washington."

"That's right, Teenie," said various members as they
sat on the curbing playing an interesting game of craps.

"Then here we is 'til Christmas, fellas; after that, this
sonny's going to move, sho, here me?"

"The gang's with you, General, move it is."

It was about a week before Christmas. The weather
had been unusually severe.

Probably because misery loves company — nothing
could be more miserable than his cat — the General
grew very fond of Tommy. He would cuddle him in his
arms every night and listen to his soft purring while he
confided all his own hopes and fears to the willing ears
of his four-footed companion, occasionally poking his
ribs if he showed any signs of sleepiness.

But one night poor Tommy froze to death. The
General didn't — more's the wonder.

Poor Tommy was thrown off the dock into the

Potomac the next morning, while a stream of salt water trickled down his dirty face, making visible, for the first time in a year, the yellow hue of his complexion.

After that the General hated all flesh and grew morose and cynical.

Just about a week before Tommy's death, the General met the fairy. Once, before his mammy died, she had forced him to go to school in a spasm of reform, urging the teacher to go up and "wallop" her child every day if he thought the General needed it. This gracious offer was declined with thanks.

At the end of the week the General left school for his own good and the good of the school. But in that week he learned something about fairies, and this was certainly one.

Being Christmas week, the General was pretty busy. It was a great sight to see the crowds of people coming and going all day long about the busy market; wagonloads of men, women and children, some carts drawn by horses, but more by mules. Some of the people well-dressed, some scantily clad, but all intent on getting enjoyment out of this, their leisure season. This was the season for selling crops and settling the year's account. The store-keepers, too, had prepared their most tempting wares for the crowds.

"I declare to the Lord, I'm done busted my ole man, sure," said one woman to another as they paused to exchange greetings outside a store door.

"Never mind," returned the other, "he'll work for more. This is Christmas, honey."

"To be sure," answered the first speaker, with a flounce of her ample skirts.

Meanwhile her husband pondered the advisability of purchasing a mule, feeling in his pockets for the price demanded, but finding them nearly empty.

"Ole mule," he said, "I want you mighty bad, but you'll have to slide this time; it's christmas, mule."

The wise old mule actually seemed to laugh as he whisked his tail against his bony sides and steadied himself on his three good legs.

The vendors were very busy, and their cries were wonderful for ingenuity of invention to attract trade:

"Hello, there, in the cellar, I've got fresh eggs for the occasion; now's your time for egg-nog with new eggs in it."

There were the stalls, too, kept by venerable aunties and filled with specimens of old-time southern cheer: Coon, cornpone, possum fat and hominy. There was piles of gingerbread and boiled chestnuts, heaps of walnuts and roasting apples. There were great barrels of cider, not to speak of something stronger. There were terrapin and persimmon in close proximity to succulent spare-ribs, sausage and crackling, savory souvenirs of the fine art of hog-killing.

And everywhere were faces of dusky hue. Washington's great negro population bubbled over in every direction.

The General was peddling chitlins. He had a tub upon his head and was singing in his strong childish tones:

> *Here's your chitlins, fresh an sweet,*
> *Young hog's chitlins hard to beat,*
> *Methodist chitlins, jest been boiled,*
> *Right fresh chitlins, they ain't spoiled,*
> *Baptist chitlins by the pound,*
> *As nice chitlins as ever was found.*

"Here, boy, does you mean to say they is real Baptist chitlins, sho nuff?"

"Yes, ma'm."

"How does you work that out?"

"The hog was raised by Mr. Robberson, a hard-shell Baptist, ma'm."

"Well, lemme have two pounds."

"Now," said a solid-looking man as the General finished waiting on a crowd of women and men, "I want some of the Methodist chitlins you've been hollering 'bout."

"Here they is, suh."

"You took 'em all outta the same tub?"

"Yes, suh. Only there's little more water on the Baptist chitlins, and they're whiter than the Methodist chitlins."

"How you tell 'em?"

"Well, suh, there's two hog's chitlins in this tub, and one of the hogs was raised by Unc' Bemis, and he's a Methodist, if that don't make him a Methodist hog nothing will."

"Weigh me out four pounds."

In an hour's time the General had sold out.

Suddenly at his elbow he heard a voice.

"Boy, I want to talk to you."

The fairy stood beside him. She was a little girl about his own age, well wrapped in costly velvet and furs. Her long, fair hair fell about her like an aureole of glory. A pair of gentle blue eyes set in a sweet, serious face glanced at him from beneath a jaunty hat with a long curling white feather that rested light as thistle-down upon the beautiful curly locks.

The General could not move for staring, and as his wonderment grew his mouth was extended in a grin that revealed the pearly whiteness of two rows of ivory.

"Boy, shake hands."

The General did not move. How could he?

"Don't you hear me?" asked the fairy, imperiously.

"Yes," replied the General meekly. " 'Deed, missy, I'm 'tirely too dirty to touch them clothes of yourn."

Nevertheless he put forth timidly and slowly a small paw begrimed with the dirt of the street. He looked at the hand and then at her. She looked at the hand and then at him. Then their eyes meeting, they laughed the sweet laugh of the free-masonry of childhood.

"I'll excuse you this time, boy," said the fairy, graciously, "but you must remember that I wish you to wash your face and hands when you are to talk with me; and," she added, as though inspired by an afterthought, "it would be well for you to keep them clean at other times, too."

"Yes," replied the General.

"What's your name, boy?"

"General Washington," he answered, standing at attention as he had seen the police do in the courtroom.

"Well, General, don't you know you've told a story about the chitlins you've just sold?"

"Told a story?" queried the General with a knowing look. "I got to sell my chitlins ahead of the other fellas, or lose my trade."

"Don't you know it's wicked to tell stories?"

"How come so?" asked the General, twisting his bare toes about in his rubbers, and feeling very uncomfortable.

"Because, God says we mustn't."

"Who's he?"

The fairy gasped in astonishment.

"Don't you know who God is?"

"Nope; never seed him. Do he live in Washington?"

"Why, God is your Heavenly Father, and Christ was His son. He was born on Christmas Day a long time ago. When He grew to be a man, wicked men nailed Him to the cross and killed Him. Then He went to heaven, and we'll all live with Him some day if we are good before we die. Oh I love Him; and you must love Him, too, General."

"Now look here, missy, you can't make this chile believe nothing like that."

The fairy went a step nearer the boy in her eagerness.

"It's true. Just as true as you live."

"Where'd you say He lived?"

"In heaven," replied the child, softly.

"What kinda place is heaven?"

"Oh, beautiful."

The General stared at the fairy. He worked his toes faster and faster.

"Say, can you have plenty to eat up there?"

"Oh, yes. You'll never be hungry there."

"And a fire, and clothes?" he queried in suppressed, excited tones.

"Yes. It's all love and plenty when we get to heaven, if we are good here."

"Well, missy, that's a powerful good story, but I'm blamed if I believe it." The General forgot his politeness in his excitement. "And if it's true, it's only for white folks; you won't find any nigger there."

"But you will; and all I've told you is true. Promise me to come to my house on Christmas morning and see my mother. She'll help you, and she will teach you more about God. Will you come?" she asked eagerly, naming a street and number in the most aristocratic quarter of Washington. "Ask for Fairy, that's me. Say quick; here comes my nurse."

The General promised.

"Lawd, Miss Fairy, honey; come right here. I'll tell your mama how you've done run away from me to talk to this dirty little monkey. Picking up such trash to talk to."

The General stood in a trance of happiness. He did not mind the slurring remarks of the nurse and even refrained from throwing a brick at the buxom lady, which was a sacrifice on his part. All he saw was the glint of golden curls in the winter sunshine and the tiny hand waving him goodbye.

"And her name really is Fairy! Just to think how I knew it all by my lonesome."

Many times that week the General thought and puzzled over Fairy's words.

"Heaven's where God lives," he would sigh. "Plenty to eat, warm fire all the time in winter, plenty of clothes', too, but I've got to be good. S'pose that means keeping my face and hands clean and stop swearing and lying. It can't be did."

The gang wondered what had come over the General.

The day before Christmas dawned clear and cold. There was snow on the ground. Trade was good and the General, mindful of the visit next day, had bought a pair of secondhand shoes and a new calico shirt.

"Get onto the dude," sang one of the gang as the General emerged from the privacy of the dry-goods box early Christmas Eve.

The General was a dancer and no mistake. Down at Dutch Dan's place they kept the old-time Southern Christmas moving along in hot time until the dawn of Christmas Day stole softly through the murky atmosphere. Dutch Dan's was the meeting place of the worst characters, white and black, in the capital city. From that vile den issued the twin spirits murder and robbery as the early winter shadows fell. There the criminal entered in the early dawn and was lost to the accusing eye of justice.

There was a dance at Dutch Dan's on Christmas Eve and the General was sent for to help amuse the company.

The shed-like room was lighted by oil lamps and flaring pine torches. The center of the apartment was reserved for dancing. At one end, the inevitable bar stretched its yawning mouth like a monster awaiting his victims. A long wooden table was built against one side of the room, where the game could be played to suit the taste of the most expert devotee of the fickle goddess.

The room was packed, early as it was, and the General's entrance was the signal for a shout of welcome. Old Unc' Jasper was tuning his fiddle and blind Remus was drawing Sweet chords from an old banjo. They glided softly into the music of the Mobile shuffle.

The General began to dance like a true master of the various styles. 'The pigeon-wing', 'the old buck', 'the hoe-down' and the 'Juba' followed each other in rapid succession. The crowd shouted and cheered and joined in the sport. There was hand-clapping and a rhythmic accompaniment of patting the knees and stamping the feet.

The General danced faster and faster while the crowd sang:

> *Juba up and juba down,*
> *Juba all around the town.*

Can't you here the juba pat?
Juba!

The General gave fresh graces and new embellishments.
Occasionally he added to the interest by yelling:
   "Ain't this fine!"
   "Oh, my!"
   "Now I'm gitting loose!"
   "Hold me, hold me!"
The crowd went wild with delight.

The child danced until he fell exhausted to the floor.
Someone in the crowd passed the hat. When all had
been waited upon the bar-keeper counted up the
receipts and divided fair — half to the house and half to
the dancer.

The fun went on, and the room grew more crowded.
General Washington crept under the table and curled
himself up like a ball. He was lucky, he told himself
sleepily, to have so warm a berth that cold night. His
heart glowed as he thought of tomorrow and Fairy, and
wondered if what she had said was true. Heaven must
be a fine place if it could beat the floor under the table
for comfort and warmth. He slept.

The fiddle creaked, the dancers shuffled. Rum went
down their throats and wits were befogged. Suddenly
the General was wide awake with a start. What was
that?

"The family are all away tonight at a dance, and the
servants gone home. There's no one there but an old
man and a kid. We can be well out of the way before the

alarm is given. 'Leven sharp, Doc. And, look here, what's the number again?"

The General knew in a moment that mischief was brewing, and he turned over softly on his side, listening mechanically to catch the reply. It came. The General sat up. He was wide awake now. They had given the street and number of Fairy's home.

Senator Tallman was from Maryland. He had owned slaves, fought in the Civil War on the Confederate side, and at its end had been returned to a seat in Congress after reconstruction, with feelings of deeply rooted hatred for the Negro. He openly declared his purpose to oppose their progress in every possible way. His favorite argument was disbelief in God's handiwork as shown in the Negro.

"You argue, suh, that God made 'em. I have my doubts, suh. God made man in His own image, suh, and that being the case, suh, it is clear that he had no hand in creating niggers A nigger, suh, is the image of nothing but the devil."

He also declared in his imperious, haughty, Southern way:

"The South is in the saddle, suh, and she will never submit to the degradation of Negro domination. Never, suh."

The Senator was a picture of honored age and solid comfort seated in his velvet armchair before the fire of blazing logs in his warm, well-lighted study. His lounging coat was thrown open, revealing its soft silken lining, his feet were thrust into gaily embroidered fur-lined slippers. Upon the baize covered table beside him, a silver salver sat holding a decanter, glasses and fragrant mint, for the Senator loved the beguiling sweetness of a mint julep at bedtime. He had been writing a speech which in his opinion would bury the blacks too deep for resurrection and settle the Negro question forever.

Just now he was idle; the evening paper was folded across his knees, a smile was on his face. He was alone in the grand mansion, for the festivities of the season had begun and the family were gone to enjoy a merry-making at the house of a friend.

There was a picture in his mind of Christmas in his old Maryland home in the 'good old days' before the war. He recalled the great ballroom where giggling girls and matrons fair glided in the stately minuet. It was in such a gathering he had met his wife, the beautiful Kate Channing.

Ah, the happy time of youth and love!

The house was very still. How loud the ticking of the clock sounded. Just then a voice spoke beside his chair:

"Please, sah, I'm General Washington."

The Senator bounded to his feet with an exclamation "Eh! Bless my soul, boy, where did you come from?"

"If you please, boss, through the window."

The Senator rubbed his eyes and stared hard at the extraordinary figure before him. The General closed the window and then walked up to the fire, warmed himself in front, then turned around and stood with his legs wide apart and his shrewd little gray eyes fixed upon the man before him.

The Senator was speechless for a moment, then he advanced upon the intruder with a roar warranted to make a six-foot man quake in his boots:

"Through the window, you black rascal. Well, I reckon you'll go out through the door, and that in quick time, you little thief."

"Please, boss, it ain't me; it's Jim the crook and the gang from Dutch Dan's."

"Eh?!" said the Senator again.

"What's your cronometer say now, boss? 'Leven is the time for the performance to begin. I reckoned I'd get here time 'nuff for you to call the police."

"Boy, do you mean for me to understand that burglars are about to raid my house?" demanded the Senator, a light beginning to dawn upon him.

The General nodded his head.

"That's it, boss, if by 'burglars' you means Jim the crook and Dutch Dan."

It was ten minutes of the hour by the Senator's watch. He went to the telephone, rang up the captain of the nearest police station and told him the situation. Then he took a revolver from a drawer of his desk and advanced toward the waiting figure before the fire.

"Come with me. Keep right straight ahead through that door. If you attempt to run I'll shoot you."

They walked through the silent house to the great entrance doors and there awaited the coming of the police. The officers surrounded the house. Silently they crept up the stairs into the now darkened study.

'Eleven' chimed the little silver clock on the mantel. There was the stealthy tread of feet a moment after, whispers, the flash of a dark lantern, a rush by the officers and a stream of electricity flooded the room.

"It's the nigger did it," shouted Jim the crook, followed instantly by the sharp crack of a revolver.

General Washington felt a burning pain shoot through his breast as he fell unconscious to the floor. It was all over in a moment. The officers congratulated themselves on the capture they had made — a brace of daring criminals badly wanted by the courts.

When the General regained consciousness, he lay upon a soft, white bed in Senator Tallman's house. Christmas morning had dawned, clear, cold and sparkling; in the air the joy-bells sounded sweet and strong: 'Rejoice, your Lord is born'.

Faintly from the streets came the sound of merry voices:

"Christmas gift, christmas gift."

The child's eyes wandered aimlessly about the unfamiliar room as if seeking and questioning. The Senator and Fairy sat beside him, a glorious stream of yellow sunshine fell upon the thorn-crowned Christ hung over the mantel.

> *God of Nazareth, see!*
> *Before a trembling soul*
> *Unfoldeth like a scroll*

Thy wondrous destiny!

The General struggled to a sitting position with arms outstretched, then fell back with a joyous, awesome cry:

"It's Him! It's Him!"

"Oh General," sobbed Fairy, "don't you die, you're going to be happy all the rest of your life. Grandpa says so."

"I was in time, little Missy. I tried mighty hard after I knowed what them devils was a-coming to."

Fairy sobbed. The Senator wiped his eyeglasses and coughed. The General lay quite still a moment, then turned himself again on his pillow to gaze at the pictured Christ.

"I'm a-gitting sleepy, missy, it's so warm and comfortable here. 'Pears like I feel right happy since I seed Him."

The morning light grew brighter. The face of the Messiah looked down as it must have looked when He was transfigured on Tabor's heights. The ugly face of the child wore a strange, sweet beauty. The Senator bent over the quiet figure with a gesture of surprise.

The General had obeyed the call of One whom the winds and waves of stormy human life obey. His Christmas Day was spent in heaven.

For some reason, Senator Tallman never made his great speech against the Negro.

AUNT RIA'S TEN DOLLARS
Georgia F. Stewart

"Ria, I hate to ask you, but can't you give me them ten dollars what you've been saving all this long time?"

"Who that? You, Lije? You got back mighty soon. I hope and trust your quick settlement was a good'un. I'll be there presently. These greens'll sho' be good and greasy when they're cooked. What you say 'bout ten dollars? That all you got in the settling with them six five hundreds?"

Elijah Davis had gone from home that morning with six bales of cotton, weighing five hundred pounds each, and his wife had been looking forward to his return, though not so early, with a great deal of anxiety. All this year she had guarded ten dollars which represented their income from eight bales the previous year, hoping to increase the sum with this year's receipts.

Elijah seated himself on the block of oak at the door, on which was a tin basin which he and Maria used for bathing their faces. There was another of smaller size beside it for the use of the little ones, of whom there were six, ranging from four months to nine years.

After pressing down the greens, which seemed to prefer any place to the kettle in which they were boiling, Maria put more fresh coals on the cover of the oven, which contained the bread. Before joining her husband she turned to the other side of the chimney which was five feet wide and, from a large oven about the size of a half bushel measure, she took two dozen sweet potatoes, put them on a large tin and left them on the hearth to cool.

"What you want? Bread? Eat them 'taters while I'm talking to your daddy."

This remark was addressed to the children, who realised the hour.

"Come out in the shade, Ria. Too hot to talk business in there."

"The weather 'pears cool to me. I been feeling like a chill all this morning. You know my mind, and yourn, too, is full of suspicions, but somehow I couldn't help saying to myself, 'this cool air make me feel uneasy 'bout Lije'. Ain't that foolish for me who attends so many good meetings at the church and up to the school with all the good books and papers read to us an', oh, the fine talks of the folks from the North."

"Go long with it, Lije. I'm ready now."

With this she smoothed her clean check apron, which she had drawn from its accustomed hook as she passed from the house, and her soiled one left in its place, and folded her hands in her lap.

"You're a woman what likes things done right. I always was proud of you. If you remember — and you is too business-fied to forget — year 'fore this last, seven bales fetch us out twenty-five dollars behind, but there was plenty corn to last for stock and all. See?"

"Yes, but —"

"Now to get the understanding, lemme finish. Last year the crop remounted to eight bales. All the back debts was paid and Mister Bradley said: " 'Lijah Davis, you're the first man this year to come out and have cash in your hands. A red cross goes down by yo' name."

"Yes, and since then, Ria Davis been holding them ten dollars, and keeping count on all that comes from Mister Bradley's store, too. Listen to me, now. 'Two piece of check for me and the chillun, five dollars; one piece o' sheet'n, two dollars; for pair shoes, five dollars; That's twelve dollars and er —"

"Well, I promise to be back soon with the ten dollars, 'cause I knowed you didn't want no accounts laid over to next year, and so I respect your feelings and come to explain matters to you."

"Where's the ten dollars you talking 'bout?"

"Your ten dollars, Ria. It's the best step to take, if you want to have clean 'count Christmas day."

"Lije Davis, them ten dollars is now part of me, and I specks for it to stay so. You and Mister Bradley been doing your kind of settling every year, and you can do it the same this year."

"Folks always called you a sensible woman, now

then don't lose yo' rep. 'Tain't no use putting your
hands akimbo and marching up and down like your
mind is made up to argufy. Be calm. All I can do is to
stick to the plough 'n make the chillun stick to the
books; so there'll be somebody else to figure 'long with
Mister Bradley. What you doing, Ria? Is you going
down with me?"

"I'm going to war. I oughta been gone years ago."

About four o'clock in the afternoon Mr. William Lyons,
a young lawyer of the town of Milton, was seated in his
office, reviewing the day and congratulating himself on
his success, when someone rapped at the door. The face
which responded to his "Enter!" was indeed a familiar
one, much to his surprise.

"Well! Well! How have you been, Aunt Maria, and
what brings you here?"

She curtsied, and began by laying the ten dollars on
his desk, and giving its history along with her trials for
the past years, since she and Elijah had been working
for themselves.

"You know 'bout the mortgage system. Every time
you feel you gitting free, sump'n come over you and
press you down again. When I felt today like my heart
going break to part with this money, Miss Ad'line's, you
dear mother's words, I remembered, and so I've come to
you. She told me never to suffer, but to go to her
William, and he would help me. Now, Mister William,
all I wants is a patch of my own, and this ten dollars'll
pay you for letting me have it; and when I raise my crop

I'll pay you for the land."

"Sit down and rest yourself, Aunt Maria. In a few moments I shall be back."

Aunt Maria was very tired, as she had walked seven miles. While she rested on one of the comfortable chairs, everything in the office seemed to breathe comforting messages to her. She determined then and there that her ambition would assert itself; that she would not wait for the children, but would do her part towards educating them — she would make a home for them.

On Mr. Lyon's return he read to Aunt Maria as follows:

"For and in consideration of ten dollars paid to me this twenty-ninth day of November, 1899, by Maria Davis, I, William Lyons, do hereby sell, grant and convey to said Maria Davis, her heirs and assigns, two acres of farming land..."

On her way home she stopped to speak to Mr. Bradley, telling him what she had done, and that the ten dollars had gone to pay for her land, but that she would pay him if he would trust her. He willingly accepted her word as guarantee of the payment.

When she reached home she unwrapped the paper, and said to Elijah, "Here's my ten dollars, to have and to hold two acres of farming land. You must set to work to get out the timbers tomorrow morning."

The distance to Simon Reese's, the nearest neighbor, was not less than two miles, but the joy of her new possessions had made the distance much less for Aunt Maria this evening. The news, which was too good to keep, was hailed with delight by the Reese family.

"When a good woman like you set her heart on doing sump'n, the Lord'll help her. Ain't nothing left here but a little scrap cotton, and I can pick that over myself; then I'll start Simon and the boys over there by daylight. Good night, Sis Ria. God help you."

Meanwhile Elijah had not been idle. His plans had been made while he watched the house and the children.

Squire Evans had used Elijah and his team at odd times during the year, in consideration of which he had promised to run the plow for him in the spring. At early dawn next morning Elijah went over to Squire Evans', a distance of three miles, and arranged for help in getting out timber instead of ploughing.

"I 'spect you have to bake right sharp bread, Ria, 'cause Squire Ivins lemme have four hands today."

"What you say? Lawd bless me! Ain't it s'prising what ten dollars can do when it starts to working? All year it was just a lone ten dollars, and now in two days it done get to be two acres of farming land. Bre'r Simon Reese and his two boys for the whole day, and four good hands from Squire Ivins!"

"Sis Ria! Oh, Sis Ria!"

"Get me some more trash chillun; this dinner oughta been gone, for now the sun at twelve o'clock, already."

"Oh, Sis Ri-a-h-!"

"Hush. I hear 'em calling me."

"Sis Ria!"

" 'Pon my soul, if that ain't Sis Reese. Step over and

come along, chile."

"Just come here to the fence, Sis Ria."

Aunt Maria had just patted in the last 'pone' of bread, and heaped her 'lid' with coals.

"All right, Sis Reese, but I'm powerful rushed."

She immersed her hands in a basin of cold water, which caused the cornmeal dough to fall from them, for she used her hands from beginning to finish in preparing the lovely oval-shaped 'pones'. On reaching the fence she had finished wiping her hands on the bottom of her apron.

"I just ran across the field to fetch you some dinner, to help you out. I dunno if you know'd it, but Simon stepped over to see Bre'r Collins and Bre'r Ha'is, this morning, and 'bout them t'aint no need to explain, 'cause they split 'nuff boards in a day to cover Miss Ad'line's big house, and they can eat accordingly."

With this she handed over a pail and a bag.

"Those are mighty fine, juicy, yaller yams, and you'll see, for short, the bread, I just dropped in the pot and boiled it all together."

"The good angel sent you here today. Hhmmm! It smells good."

"Here's you dinner, 'Lije. This is a lovely place to rest, against the fence, under these shade trees."

Aunt Maria, with the assistance of two of the children, had brought down the dinner. Both quantity and quality delighted the men, as they beheld the feast.

Parson Davis, as his neighbors commonly called him,

had never failed to ask a blessing upon the scantiest meal. Now, standing in the shade of the sweet-gum trees, he took Aunt Ria's hand in his, and raising his eyes to Heaven, gave God thanks for what was truly a feast of Thanksgiving.

THE WOOING OF PASTOR CUMMINGS
Georgia F. Stewart

"Whoa! How do you feel this morning, Brother Olmstead?"

"Well, just tolerable. You looks well and happy, but such a good man always gits along."

"Step in Brother Olmstead, I suppose you are on your way to church. How I wish they all were as true to their church as you are."

"Yes, they can all say what they please, but I said it first and I says it last, you're the man to lead this congregation — a man what education don't make too high-strung to reach down and help a poor man to a seat in his carriage. I dunno another one would take notice of me hobbling along here. They find it a mohenjus crime to speak to a poor man like me; and as for setting 'long side me like I'm by you, well I'm never going to smell that."

Reverend E. Z. Cummings, as he always signed his

name, had created between his congregation, which was composed of good, honest people, and what he termed "educated niggers", an impassable chasm.

Shortly after his settlement in this parish, he said to some of the officers of his church:

"I should not be with you long, were I to listen to people who appear to be friendly to this church."

He often intimated to them that they were considered an ignorant body, and were not worthy of an educated minister, but he would pledge himself never to leave them if they would support him in the many battles that must inevitably be fought. Being naturally pessimistic, they needed little argument to confirm his statement.

Now, the true state of affairs was this: Rev. E. Z. Cummings lacked strength of character. Soon after his invasion into a community this quality asserted itself, and he was invariably requested to resign his pastorate. Yet, in the face of this, his next victims would receive glowing reports of his last congregation.

"We missed you at prayer-meeting Friday evening, Brother Olmstead."

"You musta knowed I intended to go amongst these folks what raise this disturbment and see how the land lays. I believes you're a honorable man, I does, and if Miss Mandy Lucas whats a spreading all the talk 'bout you and certain parties was a christian whats not jealous, the population would soon stop pointing at you."

For sometime the critics had not dealt gently with

Rev. E. Z. Cummings, and the sentiment he feared was not favorable to him. He had always been able to lead his flock to the water and generally force the majority to take a drink regardless of their will. With that thought in mind, he determined to fortify himself as strongly as possible. He consciously misled every woman who would accept his attentions and give ear to his flattery, assuring each that she was his choice and the one whom he most desired for a companion.

"Here we are at the church," he said.

"Jus a minute, Reverend. I was saying that my gal Lucy Ann what is so sort of easy in her way 'bout attending Meeting and all, might some day suit the fancy of some educated shepherd. She's a likely gal, she is."

He had no idea that this introduction came entirely too late, and that the pastor had already shown his daughter much attention; which accounted for her constant attendance at the services.

"I must confess that her admirable qualities have attracted me since first I met her," said the pastor.

This Sunday was one which called into use all of the summer apparel. As a special meeting always meant a new gown for the 'sisters', a gorgeous array of cheap muslins, flowers, and ribbons met the pastor's eye, as he strode forth with lordly air, that they might be inspired by his presence, while he stood with compressed lips and bowed head, as if communing with the saints. Finally he said:

"If it were not for faith, how could we stand the

persecutions of our fellow men. Day after day I have walked meekly on and said nothing. Now, today, I offer myself to this body of brothers and sisters who have ever supported me, and for which I am thankful. Though I have been persecuted by man, right will prevail. I love every member of this church. I love to eat with them, sleep with them, and pray with them every day of my life."

"Amen! I knowed he was a innocent man from the start."

"Love to be with us poor creatures. Ain't he good."

"You been sent to lead us."

"I means to stand by you."

"Lemme shake your hand."

Such expressions came from all parts of the church. "Now my dears," the pastor continued, "before we go farther, let us give thanks for this privilege of assembling, believing that the Lord will make it alright."

At the end of three minutes of silence the pastor began singing softly:

A little more talk with Jesus makes it right, alright!
A little more talk with Jesus makes it right, alright.
In trouble of every kind, thank God I always find,
That a little talk with Jesus makes it right, alright.

Shouting and weeping were indulged in very freely while the pastor, with folded arms, walked slowly back and forth across the rostrum. One sister, as she looked up at him said, "Too good! Too good, for this earth."

Elder Jackson came forward at this juncture, and placing a small table just at the end of the centre aisle, told them in a few words that he knew they were anxious to give the pastor substantial signs of their high esteem of him.

"We are much in need of finance, and if you will march right up to the table and put down your dues, it will relieve our dear pastor, who feels the responsibility of all debts connected with the church. Will the choir please give us some music? Then you shall have a chance to come up while some of the sisters sing. Come right along now, and as soon as this is done, Reverend Eli McLemore will give us a stirring talk on the 'Agonies of Christ', since our beloved pastor is not well."

"Still we lack four dollars. We must give him fifty dollars tonight. That's right, Brother Williams. Now we need three more. Ah, here come two sisters and two brothers. Thank you, thank you, thank you. Just twenty-five cents and all will be over. Won't some dear sister give five cents of that? There, three, four, five, six sisters. That's good, a little more doesn't matter."

The minister drew from his pocket a small bag which showed signs of dust as well as wear, and handed it to the deacon. Into this bag the money was put and it was left on the floor by the pulpit where the Reverend could pick it up on going out.

Brother McLemore's talk, picturing the sufferings of Christ, served only to increase the excitement which began earlier in the service. The effect of his appeals to

them to adhere to one who had suffered for them were
tragic beyond description. Some ran to and fro, shaking
hands; some wept and walked while those who were
less demonstrative sat swaying their bodies from side to
side to the accompaniment of piteous moans, which
would signify to a listener, the loss of the last beloved
one. Then there were those who felt 'uplifted' and chose
to walk on the benches rather than on the floor, thinking
nothing of walking from the pulpit to the door stepping
from the back of one bench to another, and so on.

Another spiritual feast was yet in store for them. It
was the feast of spiritual re-enforcement. Instead of
having love-feast on Friday night of the next week, the
pastor, who arranged all things, considered it
strengthening to his reinstatement to have it associated
as closely as possible with this meeting; so he
announced it for the following evening.

It was at love-feast that all ill-feelings towards sister
or brother were obliterated; hands were shaken as bits
of bread were exchanged, and love reigned supreme.

"Sis Hannah, what you going to do 'bout Sis
Ang'line Skinner? Somehow I don't believe with all her
religion, she'll break bread with you."

"I'm going to do my duty. I have no malice in my
heart. Long ago the pastor showed his preference for Sis
Lucy Ann Olmstead. You see all comes for the best
anyhow. It ain't my nature to settle down to married life
so early."

"Chile, everybody sees you're getting ole but you.
You got just enough learning to put on stylish airs."

This exchange of words was between Miss Hannah Gibbs and Miss Maria Middleton, two maiden ladies whose modesty and generosity were potent actors in constraining them to remain in a state of being single. This was the evening for love-feast. The church was crowded.The entire congregation rose and began to break bread with each other, while all joined in singing the following:

> Won't we have a happy time
> There's a love-feast in' Heaven By'n Bye.
> My Redeemer, My Redeemer,
> There's a love-feast in Heaven By'n Bye."

> There's a love-feast in Heaven By'n Bye,
> Eating of the honey and drinking of the wine,
> There's a love-feast in Heaven By'n Bye.
> My Redeemer, My Redeemer,
> There's a love-feast in Heaven By'n Bye.

By this time Sister Hannah Gibbs had made her way to the altar, as that seemed the destination of all. They were packed so closely now that, as they rocked back and forth, keeping time to the tune of the familiar song which was interspersed with cries from the sisters who were happy, they looked like one large body being drawn from right to left, and between each vibration came a curtsy which too was strictly in keeping with the melody of the song. Here she was face to face with Sister Skinner, who for weeks had lifted her skirts and held high her head to avoid contact, not even a glance at the former. "May the good Lord bless you, Sister Skinner," and with this she forced a crumb of bread into Sister Skinner's hand, holding out her own to receive the token of good feeling. She took advantage of the opportunity to say, "Can't anybody see where the Reverend's affection is centered? On nobody but Sister Lucy Ann Olmstead."

They shook hands, exchanged bits of bread and passed on to others. During the evening the pastor was continually receiving assurances of their appreciation for him.

As the crowd left the church they were full of the feast, but among them was one whose heart was heavy. Sister Skinner had hoped that her daughter would be the fortunate one, and had begun to feel confident that he would soon ask Miss Skinner to share his home.

"It's a monstrous undertaking, but today I goes over to Sis Olmstead's to learn the facts," said Sister Skinner, after waiting several weeks for the minister's decided action in the matter.

"How you do, Sis Skinner, I dunno how come I didn't fling this water on you, because nobody never comes round that side of the house."

"Ah, sort of so so. The sickness and trouble amongst folks seems mighty rapid. Did you know Sis Mat Shepard is mighty poorly? I felt like you might want to go see her, so I just stopped to tell you I'm going to see her, and get my clothes on my way back home. It wouldn't do to miss drying clothes a day like this."

"Soon as I gits a mouthful of coffee I'll be ready," said Mrs. Olmstead.

"What you going to do today? Wash I suppose?" asked Mrs. Skinner.

"No, Lucy Ann'll wash, I have to do some sewing today. From all that I can see the Reverend will take her to his home soon, and if there is anything I hates, it's to see a nice gal go from her home short of clothes an quilts."

"Yes, you're exactly right, Sis Olmstead," said Sister Skinner, as if she knew the particulars.

It was not her plan to ask questions, but to wait until the spirit moved Sister Olmstead and she would know all. This she did.

After ministering to the sick according to their ability, they parted, Sister Skinner going for her clothes while Sister Olmstead went down to do a little trading. A few days later, Brother Olmstead met the pastor as he was driving along the street.

"Reverend, I want to talk with you."

"Whoa, how do you feel this morning, Brother Olmstead?"

"No good feelings towards you. What you mean by fooling with my gal? All the time I've been working for you, even to rushing in the enemy's camp, she seemed powerful pleasing to your choice amongst all the fine flowers, and now when your foundation quit rocking and all appears peaceful, you just say to her: 'It ain't prudent for me to take that step'. Lemme tell you, man, you done break her heart, let alone how me and her mammy done strain the last notch to get articles what's suitable for that position. Lucy Ann's not the same. The poor chile never will care for nobody else. Her face done drop down like them sisters on the hill. All she need is the veil, but I trust she never takes it."

Brother Olmstead was not be toyed with, and the reverend saw it; so drove off rapidly, saying that he would see him again.

A church meeting had been appointed for the next evening. This bit of news had spread through the village, and behind it followed brother Olmstead arousing the sympathy of all he met. When the subject was introduced at the meeting it was amazing how many people accused the Reverend of the same thing. Brother Olmstead told those assembled, if they did not dismiss the pastor that he would put him out by force. It was decided by the majority that he be required to seek work elsewhere immediately.

Thus the Reverend E. Z. Cummings passed from this active field of labor.

THE OCTOROON'S REVENGE
Ruth D. Todd

He was a tall young fellow, with the figure of an athlete, extremely handsome, with short black curls and dark eyes.

His companion was a beautiful girl, tall and slight, though exceedingly graceful, with masses of silken hair of a raven blackness, and with eyes large and dreamy, of a deep violet blue.

But while she was the daughter of one of Virginia's royal blue bloods, he was simply a young mulatto coachman in her father's employ.

The young girl was sitting on a mossy bank by the side of a shady brook while the young man lay at her feet. A carriage with a pair of fine horses stood just at the edge of the wood, across the roadway.

At last the young man spoke, looking up at the girl as he did so, and there was a world of anguish in his sad, dark eyes.

"Lillian, dearest, I am afraid that this must be our last day alone with each other."

"Oh, Harry dear, why so, what has happened? Does any one suspect us?" exclaimed the young girl as she moved swiftly from her seat and knelt by his side.

He caught both her hands in his and covered them with kisses before he replied.

"No, dearest, nothing has happened as yet, but something may at any moment, Lillian darling." And the young man raised himself up and clasped the girl passionately to his heart. "It almost drives me mad to tell you, but I must go away."

"Oh, no. No! No! Harry, dear Harry, surely you do not mean what you are saying."

"Yes, darling, I must go. For your sake; for both of our sakes. Think dear one, it is quite possible that we may be found out some day, and then think of the shame and disgrace it will bring to you. Think what a blow it would give your father; what a blight it would cast upon an old and honored name. Shunned and despised by your most intimate friends, you would be a social outcast. They would lynch me, of course, but for myself I care not. It is of you that I must think, and of your father who has been so very kind to me. Dear heart, I would gladly lay down my life to save your pure and spotless name."

"Harry, dearest, although a few drops of Negro blood flows through your veins, your heart is as noble and your soul as pure as that of anyone of my race. I would fain take you by the hand as my own, defying friends, father — defying the world, Harry, for I love you; and if you leave me I shall surely go mad. It would break my heart, it would kill me," cried the girl, with frantic sobs.

"Oh, why was I ever born to wreck so pure and beautiful a heart as this? Why, oh, why is it such a crime for one of Negro lineage to dare to love the woman of his choice? Darling, I wish that we had never met, that I had died before seeing your beautiful face and then, dear one, you would be free to love and honor one of your own class; one who would be more worthy of you; at least, worthier than I, a Negro."

"To me, Harry, you are the noblest man on earth, and Negro that you are, I would not have you changed. I only wish, dear, that I also was possessed of Negro lineage, so that you would not think me so far above you. As it is dear — perhaps it is but the teaching of Mammy Nell — I feel something as though I belonged to your race, at any rate I shall very soon, for whither you go, there too I shall be."

"My darling, what do you mean?" he asked anxiously.

"Simply this, that we can elope!"

"Oh, Lillian, dear one, you forget that you are the daughter of one of Virginia's oldest aristocrats."

"Do not reproach me for that Harry. Have I not thought, and wept, and prayed over it until my eyes were dim and my heart ached? I tell you there is no other way. We could go to Europe. I have always longed to visit Italy and France. Oh, Harry, we could be so happy together."

"Lillian, my dearest," he cried as he drew her closer within his embrace and pressed passionate kisses on her upturned face. Then, as suddenly, he pushed her away.

"No. No. I am but mortal; do not tempt me. It would be worse than cowardly to do this. I cannot. Oh God. I cannot."

But the girl wound her beautiful arms around his neck and asked tenderly: "Not even for my sake, Harry? Not even if it was the only thing on earth that would make me happy?"

The soft arms clinging about his neck, the pleading eyes gazing into his, completely stole his senses. He could not draw her closer to him, but his voice shook with emotion as he answered.

"Lillian, I have said that I would die for you, if it would but make you happy. And the thought of taking you away and making you my wife drives me wild with joy. Will you trust yourself with me?"

"I am yours, take me to your heart," was her reply.

And he kissed her again passionately, almost madly; he called her sweetheart, wife, and many other endearing names.

A week later the country for miles around was ringing with the news of Lillian Westland's elopement with her father's Negro coachman.

A posse of men and women scoured the country for miles around hoping to find the young people established in some dainty cottage. Cries of "Lynch the Nigger! Lynch the Nigger!" rang through the woods, and many were the comments, innuendoes and slighting words bestowed upon the young girl, who had been such a pet, but who had now outraged society so grossly.

It was a terrible shock to Lillian's white-haired aristocratic father. He had loved and worshipped his beautiful daughter and only child. But this madness, this ignominious conduct that his well-beloved and petted darling had shown, crushed and dazed him, and placed him in a stupor from which it was impossible to arouse him. He shut himself up and refused to see even his most intimate friends.

The short, imploring, pitiful letter he received from Lillian, confessing all, and begging that in time her father would look upon her conduct a little less harshly, failed to animate him.

A month later, the news of the Hon. Jack Westland's death from suicide was announced by the entire press. A deep mystery was connected with the suicide, of which vague hints were published in the daily papers. But nothing definite being known, the Westland mystery was soon forgotten by the world in general.

By only one person was the key of the mystery held, and she was a servant, who had been in the Westland's employ for many years.

This servant was an octoroon woman of about thirty-five years of age. Her eyes were the most remarkable feature about her. They were large and dark, at times

wild and flashing, and again gentle and appealing,
which fact conveyed to one the idea of a most romantic
history. Her straight nose, well cut mouth and the
graceful poise of her head and neck showed that she
was once a very beautiful creature, as well as an ill-used
one, to judge from her story which was as follows.

*It was twenty years ago that I first took the position as
chambermaid at Westland Towers; I was just sixteen years of
age that day — June the 17th, 1875. My mother I never knew,
but I was told by an aunt, an only relative of mine, that my
mother had been a beautiful quadroon woman, and my father
a member of one of Virginia's best families. My aunt having
died while I was as yet but ten years old, the hardships and
misery I experienced during my wretched existence between
ten and sixteen, can better be imagined than described.*

*The filth and degradation of the low-class Negroes among
whom, for lack of means, I was forced to live, disgusted me so
that I grew to despise them. I held myself aloof from them and
refused to take part in the vulgar frivolities which they
indulged in, and occupied my spare moments in study,
thereby evoking a torrent of anger and abuse upon my head
from the lowest Negroes. It was therefore with great relief that
I accepted a position as chambermaid at Westland Towers,
preferring to live as a servant with white people than to be the
most honored guest of the Negroes among whom I had lived.
I was young then, and the blood of my father who was a great
artist, was stronger in me than that of my mother.*

Naturally I hated all things dark, loathsome and

disagreeable, and my soul thirsted and hungered for the bright sunshine and the brilliancy and splendor of all things beautiful, which I found at the Westland Towers. It was one of the most magnificently beautiful places in Virginia.

The Westland family were of old and proud descent, and consisted of a father, son and a wizened old housekeeper. The son was a handsome man. In fact I will describe him as I saw him for the first time in my life. I was in the act of dusting his private sitting room, when I turned and saw this handsome young man standing in the doorway. The expression on his face was one of ardent admiration. His violet blue eyes, as they gazed into mine seeming to read my very soul, had a charm about them which drew me to him in spite of myself. His short curls, which lay about his high aristocratic forehead shone like bright gold, and a soft, light mustache hid a mouth which was better acquainted with a smile than a sneer. His figure was tall and stalwart, though as graceful as a woman's, and altogether, he impressed me as being by far the most handsome man I had ever seen.

He spoke to me pleasantly, kindly, and with a gentleness which seemed to thrill my very soul. I was young and foolish, unused to the ways of the world and of men, and when his blue eyes looked into mine, so appealingly, and his gentle, musical voice spoke to me so tenderly, telling me that I was the most beautiful girl in all the world, and that he loved me passionately, nay madly, adding that if I would only be his, he would place me in a beautiful house with servants, horses and carriages; telling me that I should have beautiful dresses and jewelry and that all within the household should worship me, I laid my head upon his breast and told him I would be his.

But when I asked him if we could not marry he replied that it was impossible. That if he ever married one of colored blood, his father's anger would be so great as to cause his disinheritance, and that then he could not place his darling in a high position, adding that being born a gentleman, it would go hard with him to try to earn his own livelihood, all of which seemed to me a very fitting excuse. He also told me that it was not a marriage certificate or the words of a ceremony which made us man and wife. That marriages were made in Heaven, and if we loved each other and lived together, God would look down on us and bless our union, adding that he would always love me and never leave me. Oh God, that was a bitter trial. I had no mother to advise me; no friend to go to for assistance, and the very thought of giving him up for the filth and degradation from which I came, tortured me for days, during which time my great love for him overcame all obstacles, and on the 4th of July, I found myself living in the luxury of love.

We lived together for eighteen months, during which time no sorrow came to me, save the death of a baby boy. Oh they were happy days. I was assuredly the happiest girl in all Virginia But there came evil times. His father died, and of course he had to leave me for a time to attend to important duties.

I was sorry for his father's death and I was also glad, thinking that now no obstacle being in the way, he would surely marry me. But in this I was doomed to bitter disappointment.

A young and beautiful lady, a distant cousin of his, stole his heart from me, and when I received a letter from him telling me that grave duties confronted him, and though it broke his heart to say it, he must part from me, offering me an annuity of five hundred dollars, a great lump rose in my throat which seemed to choke me. I felt my heart breaking.

The things before my eyes began to dance and gloat at me in my anguish. Then everything grew dark and I knew no more for several weeks. When I regained consciousness, my first impulse was to kill myself, but remembering that in a few months I would become a mother for the second time, I stayed my hand. I also accepted the annuity of five hundred dollars, thinking that if my little one lived, it would amount to a small fortune when of age. My love died, and in its stead lived hatred and thirst for vengeance. I thought constantly of the words: Hell hath no fury like a woman scorned, and likened them unto myself.

I was young: I could be patient for years, but an opportunity presented itself sooner than I expected. Eight months before the birth of my child which was a girl, Jack Westland married, and one year after his marriage, his beautiful young wife was called away by death, the cause of which was a tiny baby girl. The death of his young wife caused him such anguish that he shut himself up and would see no one. He would not even look upon the face of the poor motherless babe. He bade the housekeeper to procure a wet nurse for the infant, which was a delicate little thing, and as there were no other to be obtained, they sought me out and begged me to take the position as nurse.

I obstinately refused at first, but on learning that Jack would soon go abroad to try and divert his mind, I accepted, for an idea that would suit my purpose exactly flashed *through my brain. The two babies were almost exactly alike, both having violet blue eyes and dark hair. Indeed the only difference between them was that my baby was four months older. Supposing that the young heiress should die? Could I not deftly change the babies? I would try at all events.*

Accordingly it was arranged that I should, as a competent nurse go to some watering place on account of the young heiress' health.

All things went as I had hoped. The young heiress as I expected died, and I mourned her death as that of my own, and when I returned to Westland Towers, no one noticed any change, but that the sea air had improved the baby's health wonderfully.

When Jack returned home two years later, he saw a beautiful, blue eyed baby girl, with jet black curls about her little neck. He greeted me kindly, but there was no touch of passion in his voice. In fact he treated me as an exalted servant which made me hate him all the more.

"He was glad," he said "that I took such an interest in the welfare of little Lillian," and he asked me if there was any special thing that he could do to repay me.

There was one thing I desired above all others, and that was the education of a mulatto lad of ten years of age, who worked about the stables. I asked him if he would send the lad to some industrial institution, which request he readily granted. There is but little more to tell. My little girl grew to be a beautiful young lady, the pet and leader among Virginia's most exclusive circle. But the teachings of her old mammy Nellie, she never forgot.

Her sympathy was always for the poor and lowly, and

though there were scores of young men of aristocratic blood seeking her heart and hand, she preferred, as I intended she should, the colored youth, Harry Stanly.

"It was the result of this little episode of the change in the babies, which I related to Jack Westwood, after the elopement, that caused him to commit suicide, and as he leaves everything to his daughter Lillian, I hope we shall live happily hereafter," said Mammy Nellie, as she arose and rung for lights.

"My poor abused mother," exclaimed both Harry and Lillian simultaneously, who had just joined her in New York City, as both threw a loving arm tenderly around her neck.

"And now," said Lillian, "your revenge is complete. Let us close up the house, and go abroad. We can remain away several years, traveling and enjoying the beauties of the Old World. What do you say to this?"

"A capital idea," said Harry.

"As well as a practical one, for even here in New York race feeling sometimes runs very high," said the octoroon avenger, with a curl of scorn about her mouth, and a triumphant light flashing from her beautiful dark eyes.

FLORENCE GREY
Ruth D. Todd

It was nearly midnight as two gentlemen left a fashionable club in one of the most prominent avenues in Washington. One of the gentlemen, by name Percy Belmont, was considered good looking, but the other, Richard Vanbrugh, was very distinguished in appearance, and withal quite handsome. But there was about him an air that proclaimed him a man of rather fast habits, despite the fact that he would soon be thirty.

His eyes were as blue as the heavens above, with a certain amount of daring lurking in the corners. And his hair, which he always wore brushed carelessly back from his white, aristocratic brow was of a chestnut brown. A rich, full mustache of the same color partly covered a beautifully cut mouth, which had about it a somewhat sarcastic expression. In stature he was above the average height, though proportionately built, and from the crown of his silk hat, to the tip of his patent leather boot, a gracefulness and an air of free and easy superiority moved with every turn of his fine figure.

"Shall we take a cab or walk, Percy?" asked Richard Vanbrugh, as both gentlemen stopped to strike a match with which to light their fragrant Havanas.

"The latter by all means," answered Percy Belmont. "A cab is too confounded close on such an evening as this. By the by, Dick, it's quite a pleasant surprise to run across you at the Arlington when I thought you were abroad."

"Thanks, Percy, my boy, but I haven't been over a week yet, and I just arrived in Washington tonight. So thinking that I might run across someone I knew at the Arlington, I stopped in."

"And right glad I am that you did, for it gives me much pleasure to be the first to welcome you back to Washington again, albeit the season is far advanced. By the way Dick, while I have you, I'd like to hear you say that you will come down to Belmont Grange and spend a few weeks with me next month."

"Thanks, nothing could give me more pleasure. Why, let's see, it's quite five years since I have been down to the Grange, isn't it, Percy?"

And both gentlemen as they walked leisurely along were so engrossed in each other's society that they failed to note which way they turned their footsteps, and suddenly found themselves in a less prominent avenue, but withal a very quiet and respectable thoroughfare.

In fact, one of the houses was brilliantly lighted, and

before the entrance stood several carriages. Just as the
gentlemen turned to retrace their footsteps, the door
was opened and several negroes with soft laughter and
pleasant adieus descended the white marble steps and
sought their different carriages.

Among the foremost was an elegant-looking matron
accompanied by a young girl who was tall, slight and
exceedingly graceful, with the beauty of a goddess. The
glare of an electric light fell full upon her face; and a
painter would have likened it unto a queen of the night.

Her complexion was very fair, so fair that she had
often been mistaken for a white girl. She had a luxuriant
growth of hair which was soft and brilliant, and as black
as night, a pair of soft, lustrous dark eyes which looked
forth innocently and frankly from 'neath long, silken
lashes; a thin, straight nose, and a sweet mouth whose
lips were as soft and as red as a blush rose. A black lace
mantilla rested lightly upon her brilliant black hair and
a lightweight evening wrap enveloped her slight form.

Her manner was gentle, sweet and very refined, and
there was a grace and elegance about her that is only
found in a gentlewoman.

Dick Vanbrugh gave an involuntary stare, thinking
to himself that of all the beautiful and charming women
he had ever seen this was by far the most beautiful as
well as the most charming young girl in all the world.

Percy Belmont did not stare at the girl, but he did
glance anxiously at Dick Vanbrugh, knowing the latter's
weakness for pretty faces.

"By Jove, Percy, what a beautiful creature."

"Yes, she is pretty," answered Percy, assuming a careless air.

Dick stared at him in infinite surprise.

"Pretty! Good Heavens, Belmont, you are quite as cold and impassive as ever. Why, she is beautiful, fascinating heavenly," he exclaimed rapturously.

Percy gave a careless laugh.

"Calm yourself, my dear Vanbrugh, or I'm afraid you'll lose your head."

Dick flushed slightly, but continued, though with less fervour.

"I'm afraid you'll think me an ass, Belmont, but I always was, you know, when a beautiful woman is the subject. But fancy calling such a lovely creature by the insignificant word 'pretty'. By George, I have half a mind to call a cab and follow our fair friend's carriage."

"That would be quite useless; she would only treat any flirtations on your part with scorn and utmost contempt, for she is considered the pink of Negro aristocracy."

Vanbrugh gave a short laugh, which was his common mode of expressing incredulity.

"By Jove, that's a capital joke. As if any colored damsel, no matter how refined or elegant she may be, would treat the attentions of a gentleman with scorn; especially if the latter is by no means bad looking and generous to a fault."

"My dear Dick, there are certain Negro families residing in Washington who are as proud as we are."

"Nonsense, I shall try this one at all events."

Percy's manner changed to one of earnestness; he laid his hand affectionately on Vanbrugh's shoulder.

"My dear fellow, you will oblige me by doing no such thing."

Vanbrugh bit his lip and waveringly asked: "No, and why?"

"Because the girl, whose name is Florence Grey, is a lady."

"Oh, you know her, then?" he asked, with slight sarcasm."

"Yes, that is — I know of her. I know of her family, too. Their summer residence is about a half mile below Belmont Grange."

"How fortunate. And, of course you will be good enough to tell me more about this fair maiden."

"With pleasure, if you will spend some time with me."

"Certainly. I'll remain with you forever if you say so," laughed Dick, now in the best of humor, as both ascended the brownstone steps leading to the entrance of Percy's fashionable boarding place.

The fashionable widow Grey was a charming mulattress. Her husband had been a wealthy white man — a Yankee who had waived all caste aside and married the woman of his choice. For many years they had lived in Europe, their two children James and Florence, being born there. But on account of his ill health, the doctor advised him to seek his native shores again. So he came to Washington and settled his family in a palatial residence where, ten years previous to the opening of this story, he died.

His widow was heartbroken, and shut herself up in seclusion for two years; at the end of which time she bestirred herself to such an extent that she was very soon the leader of Negro society. Her son James, who was a tall, handsome young man of twenty-five, had just left college, and with the prefix of Dr. to his name, bade fair to be a very interesting as well as important personage in Negro business life.

Florence, the beautiful young girl already described was twenty-two. She had finished her education, including a collegiate course, and was now doing her first full season in society.

Their country residence was quite an elegant affair, being an old two-storey, white stone mansion, whose spacious halls and apartments had been modernized and fitted up with artistic taste, displaying luxury and elegance that would be admired by the most fastidious.

They moved in, or rather led, a class of the most reputable Negroes in Washington, and in summer their country residence was filled with the elite. This, Percy Belmont made his friend acquainted with, at the same time giving him to understand that they were a class of Negroes, who generally commanded respect, adding that for Vanbrugh to try and flirt with the beautiful Florence was the most abject folly.

Vanbrugh colored deeply, but there was an expression of daring in his handsome blue eyes, as well as a determination about his whole person as he replied:

"You mean well, my dear Belmont, and I daresay I ought to take your advice but, you see, my dear boy, I have always been a shockingly bad fellow, and I fear some day that I'll go to the devil where I belong. So spare yourself any further advice and let's talk over old times."

And this conversation was never again referred to, Belmont, evidently, forgetting all about it, while on the contrary, it was impressed still more deeply on Vanbrugh's mind.

Richard Vanbrugh was born in Virginia of wealthy and aristocratic parents who died when he was a mere lad, leaving him in the care of guardians who were too strict with him, and kept him in far more closely than was at all prudent with a lad of his temperament, so that when he became of age and felt himself his own master, he fell in with a set of fast young men and led a shockingly wild life.

There was no madness, no diabolical trick that Dick Vanbrugh was not the originator of.

With women, he had always been a perfect pet; beginning from his old mammie nurse and only ending with the most fastidious society belle.

He was not exactly a prig, but from his earliest recollection women had petted and indulged him, so that it seemed only natural that those of his fancy should succumb to the charms of his handsome person, entrancing smiles and honeyed words.

And he had taken ardent fancy for this lovely colored

girl, and did not mean that she should escape him.

In a month's time everyone in Washington would be seeking places of less intense heat. The Greys would, of course, leave for their country place, and as he had accepted Belmont's invitation to join him with a company of friends at the Grange, he was content to abide his time assuring himself that with a little patience he would certainly win her in the end. Never before had he beheld the girl whom he desired so ardently, and it would be no fault of his if he did not win her love in less than three months' time.

It was a few days later, and everybody in Washington who moved in Afro-American society was discussing the greatest event of the season. A grand ball was to be given by the elegant widow Grey at her palatial residence.

It would be the best yet, and probably the closing event of a successful season.

Everybody who was anybody tried to secure invitations, for it was rumored that the ball would be given partly in honor of John Warrington, a young Northerner, a prominent young businessman staying with the Greys. And as the young man was possessed of a snug fortune, handsome person and pleasing manners, he was considered a great 'catch'.

"My dear Jack," James Grey had playfully remarked, "I'm afraid you will have to enclose your heart in a steel case, or you may go back home minus it, for our girls down here in Washington are the fairest of the fair."

"Your words are very true, in one case at least, for I think that Miss Grey, your sister, is the most beautiful young lady l have ever met."

"Thanks, Jack, yes, Florence is very pretty, and the dearest sister on earth, but to-morrow night you will see some of the fairest girls the world has ever produced."

The night of the ball finally arrived and Mrs. Grey's rooms were very beautiful indeed. Trailing evergreens and floating ferns, through the interstices of which gleamed unveiled statues, and the distant murmur of wild, sweet music caused one to marvel and wonder if they were not in some enchanted palace.

James Grey had not been exaggerating when he assured Jack Warrington that the prettiest girls the world could produce would be at the ball, for the most beautiful faces, rich dresses and rare gems flashed brightness as they moved through the spacious ballroom.

But Florence, clad in a gown of chiffon and rich lace, with a bunch of scarlet roses in her hands and one nestling amid the coils of her brilliant black hair, was by far the most beautiful woman in the room.

"Prettiest girl in Washington."

"Who, Miss Grey?"

"Certainly, of whom else do you suppose I was speaking?"

Jack Warrington, standing behind a huge exotic plant heard this conversation go on between two foppish-looking young men.

"Well, there's Sadie Payne, you know; you may have been speaking of her."

"Sadie, oh, she's the biggest flirt here."

"Probably, but there is no denying that she is pretty."

"Of course not; but of what advantage are her charms when a fellow can't get in edgeways?"

"I don't know; Jim Grey seems to be making rapid progress with his wooing."

"Well, that isn't very singular. He and Sadie were children together so the intimacy may be only friendship."

"But there is no denying that this chum of Jim's is sweet on Florence."

"By George, it's a shame. This Yankee shall not win our fairest flower without a hard struggle, for I, for one, shall be one of his antagonists. I shall go immediately to Miss Grey and beg the next dance."

Both men disappeared amid the throng.

Warrington's first impulse was to seek his friend and put this bit of gossip to a test, but on second thought he remembered that he was engaged to dance the next with Florence and he hastened to her instead.

Sadie Payne was a charming young girl. She was the only child of Mr. and Mrs. George Payne, a refined, though by no means wealthy couple, who resided about two blocks from the Greys. Mrs. Payne had been Mrs. Grey's dearest girl friend before either had married, and had always kept up the intimacy despite the fact that Mrs. Grey was exceedingly wealthy and Mrs. Payne not in the very best circumstances.

In summer, either all three or else Sadie alone had
been the guest of Mrs. Grey for two weeks or more. But
for two years they had managed somehow to build a
snug cottage not far from Mrs. Grey's summer
residence, and the young folks were seldom, if ever,
separated. It was almost a settled thing that James and
Sadie would marry some day, but though it was
gossiped with much fervor among their friends, no
engagement had ever been announced. The young lady
in question was very pretty, though by no means showy.
She was possessed of a charming figure, not very tall,
but by no means undersized, and a light brown
complexion. Her hair was black and curly and worn in
a fascinating style which she seldom, if ever, changed.
But her chief charm lay in her eyes, which were large,
bewitching, mirthful, tantalizing and as dark as night.

She was dressed in a simple gown of white organdie
and surrounded by a group of young people who were
ever at her beck and call, for being the most intimate girl
friend of Miss Florence Grey, she was a very popular
young girl.

So as the night grows old, the dances grow low down
on the cards, the waiters in their white jackets move less
frequently through the well-bred crowd, and sundry
elderly guests bid the hostess good night, feeling proud
to be the departing guests of the best and most
successful ball of the season.

It was the first of July, two months later, and the Greys,

as well as Percy Belmont, were established in their palatial summer residences.

The Greys were entertaining very few guests at present, nor few of their friends were able to take in a full season's vacation.

Jack Warrington had promised to spend a few weeks with them, but his business would not allow him to indulge in this pleasure until August, and though the guests were few, the pleasures and amusements were many, and the young folks enjoyed themselves with utmost zeal.

Though Dick Vanbrugh had tried flirting with Florence several times, as he met her alone on the highway, his wooing was progressing very slowly, or rather not progressing at all, for any advances on his part had been met with utmost scorn by that lovely young lady. Indeed, she had shown him with an uplifting of her proud head and a flash of withering contempt from the beautiful dark eyes, that he was of utmost inconsequence to her.

This had angered his vanity, but at the same time it had strengthened his desire to win her. She seemed more beautiful to him than ever, and while he was still trying to think of some plan with which to succeed, it suddenly occurred to him that what Belmont had said was true. The girl was certainly a lady, and there was something a little special about her — a little touch of hauteur that repelled while at the same time it attracted, charmed, fascinated one. And he would have given her up, but somehow it seemed that the dark, liquid eyes haunted him; he could almost feel the touch of her soft, lustrous hair. She seemed to have thrown a spell about him, which, do as he might, he was unable to shake off.

Good Heavens! Was there no way of gaining this charming girl? And if there wasn't, would he never forget her? He had been petted and spoiled by some of the most fastidious society belles, and yet, not one of them had exerted such an influence over him. Could it be that he was in love with her? He, Richard Vanbrugh, the heir and last descendant of an old and aristocratic name, in love with a Negress?

"My God," he cried, desperately. "Am I mad? Am I possessed of some strange delirium? Will I awake and find that I have been dreaming? No, oh no, it is only too true and I must tear her image from my heart and crush it," he cried, beating his breast savagely in his great anguish. He lit a cigar and strolled out to the woods to try and quiet his nerves and, having found a quiet spot some little distance from the Grange, he threw himself down disconsolately beneath the refreshing shadow of a magnificent old oak. But a feeling of discomfort had taken possession of him, and he threw his cigar to the winds and groaned aloud in anguish. What should he do? What could he do? He could not make her his wife, and he dared not try another flirtation with her for fear of losing her forever. What he would say would come from his heart. And besides he could not bear to see the beautiful eyes flash with indignation, and the proud lips curl with infinite scorn. No, no, those eyes were made to glow with passion, those lips to give forth sweetest kisses. But would they before him? A voice within him whispered: 'No, they will not. They are for one of her own blood — a Negro'.

His was a quick and passionate nature, and he was on his feet in a moment, and an expression of jealousy and fury flashed from his eyes as he clenched his fists and exclaimed aloud, "By heavens, I will not give her up."

He had been so blinded by his passion that he had not seen the long, lank form of a Negro striding leisurely down the road towards him, and when the man addressed him, he started sharply and swore a terrible oath, asking furiously:

"Who are you, and what the devil do you want?"

The colored fellow, notwithstanding his lankiness, was a rather good-looking black man, and there was an expression in his keen eyes not unlike that in Vanbrugh's. In fact, this fellow, who was called 'Long Tom' was a perfect daredevil — the terror of the Negro inhabitants down in the village. But, possessing a very pleasing manner, he smiled, showing two perfect rows of ivory teeth, bowed profusely, and answered:

"I beg the boss' pardon if I 'sprised him, but I thought you was in trouble and I might be able to assist you. My name is Long Tom, sah," and he grinned significantly.

Vanbrugh scrutinized the fellow closely. 'Long Tom', where had he heard that name before? Ah, yes, he was the devilish negro whom he had heard the fellows laughing about at the Grange. But why did the man think he could be of service to him?

"You say that your name is Long Tom, and you thought I was in trouble?" asked Vanbrugh.

The man nodded.

"You are, so I have heard, a worthless young scoundrel. So tell me, pray, why in thunder did you imagine I needed your help?"

" 'Cause I'm the only one what could do it. But I am afraid I made the boss mad, so good day, sah," and he turned to go.

"Stay," commanded Vanbrugh, as a devilish idea flashed through his brain. "Can I place confidence in you?"

"Oh, yes indeed, boss."

Vanbrugh looked him steadily in the eye for a moment, then said, "Meet me here tonight at twelve o'clock sharp. I will be waiting for you. Leave me now, and remember: Silence is golden."

Shoving a crisp bank note into the man's hand, he pushed him gently towards the roadway.

It was midnight. During the early part of the evening a heavy storm had been approaching, so that by now it was raging with all the fury of Hades. The wind blew with such cruel violence as to uproot trees and scatter destruction in its path. Great flashes of vivid lightning lit up the country for miles around and heavy thunder shook the earth with its deep and deafening roar. Accompanying this was a downpour of drenching rain,

but despite this fact, Dick Vanbrugh, the elegant
gentleman, and Long Tom, the young Negro scoundrel,
had both dared to brave its fury. Vanbrugh swearing as
he drew his long coat closer about him, that he would
brave hell itself; and Long Tom being in very destitute
circumstances, swore the same oath. So that by the time
they reached their meeting place, both were possessed
of decidedly bad tempers.

"Beastly night, this, my man," said Vanbrugh.

"Certainly is, and dangerous beneath these trees,
sah," answered Tom.

"I know, but where the devil can we go, fellow?"
asked Vanbrugh, rather sharply.

"I was thinking that the boss might not mind going
round to my shanty, a little way up the woods there; I
lives by myself."

"Anywhere out of this. Lead on."

And both men struggled on until they reached the
entrance of a lone cabin situated in the heart of the
woods. Tom unlocked the door, and pushing it open so
that Vanbrugh might enter first, apologetically said, "
'Tain't much better in here, but it's better'n being out in
the rain, though."

Dick felt like telling the fellow to go to hell, but
instead he entered the place and cast a deprecating
glance around at the few pieces of furniture (if two
chairs, a table and an old ante bellum bedstead could be
given that name) and asked Tom why the devil did he
bring him to such a beastly hole.

To which Tom replied that "It's the best place I know

about, and the gent could select a better if he has a mind to."

The elegant Richard Vanbrugh being exceedingly out of temper and growing more angry each moment, told Tom to "Shut up!" and that he wanted none of his damned insolence, adding that it would be better if he appeared more respectful in the presence of a gentleman.

And Tom, being only a low-class Negro, followed this advice.

Meanwhile, Vanbrugh lit a cigar and paced the dusty floor back and forth; presently he drew off his coat, threw it over the back of a chair and continued to pace the floor in moody silence.

By this time, the fire of pine bark and twigs which blazed on the old-fashioned hearth had sucked up the dampness of the apartment; and after a few more strides he went over to the fire and seated himself. He felt more comfortable now and in somewhat better humor.

"Well, Tom, it's about time to come to business now, unless we — that is, I — intend to remain here all night. Here is a cigar for you and, about this business?" Here Vanbrugh hesitated. It was a nasty piece of business, but must be done. 'By thunder, I hate to confide in anyone, but then, this fellow is only a Negro, and will hold his tongue for fear of getting his neck broken, and besides I must have help from someone', he told himself. Then he said to Tom:

"Tom, you must have suspected something when you came upon me so suddenly this afternoon; so fire away and let me hear all about it."

Then Tom told him that he had followed him around for several days, and learned that he was trying to get in with the wench Florence.

But here Vanbrugh interrupted him sternly, almost fiercely, bidding him never to speak lightly of that young lady again or it would be the worse for him, adding:

"Yes, I have taken a fancy for her, but there is no way on earth of winning her until she is in my power. But to accomplish that, I am afraid she will have to be abducted. And you, my man, are the only one who could do this."

Tom's keen eyes glistened like the bright orbs of some hideous reptile, but he said nothing, and Vanbrugh asked savagely, "Well, and why the devil don't you answer me?"

Long Tom grinned diabolically, rubbed his hands together and replied, "I'm thinking it's a mighty tough piece of business, and if I gits ketched it'll go mighty hard with me."

"You lie. What you want is money — and what I want is this girl Florence. You can kidnap her as easily as I can snap my fingers, and you will kidnap her if I pay you well. I will also add that money is of no consequence to me, and being very wealthy, I am always exceedingly liberal to those whom I employ. Am I plain enough, or do you wish to name your sum before you begin?"

"Oh, no, boss, no need of that 'til after I gits her for

you, and that I can do as soon as you likes."

"Very well then, here are my plans: Some time in August — I will see you later to set the date — some evening you are to kidnap this girl and, you know where the Haunted Towers are? Well, you are to bring her there, where I will have a closed carriage in readiness, and once we get her in the carriage the rest will be quite easily managed. You are to drive us to a little country place of mine some ten or fifteen miles beyond the village. But enough of the plan, I will tell you everything when I am in a better temper. Tomorrow I leave Belmont Grange; and I am to be seen by no one save you, in these parts again. And I will only see you once, which will be, let me see, on August the first, at midnight here in your cabin."

And the storm having, in the meantime, abated, Vanbrugh arose and drew on his long coat. Then, taking out his wallet, he handed Tom five or six bank notes.

"This will do you until I see you again, so au revoir," and he was soon swallowed up in the darkness without.

July had gone, and half of August. Mrs. Grey's summer residence was now filled with the most charming of guests.

It was a lovely day, being the month of August. It was hot, but not unpleasantly so, for a slight breeze, together with the refreshing shadows of the tall and wide-spreading old trees had helped to rob the day of its fervor. A party of young people had assembled together and gone to explore the ruins of the Haunted Towers, which was about three quarters of a mile from Grey's Villa.

There was a legend associated with the Haunted Towers, from which it derived its name. Many years ago, the Haunted Towers, named then Wycliffe Towers, was the principal house of the county, and gallant men and beautiful women had danced, flirted and made merry through its spacious halls and apartments.

The last master was Philip Wycliffe, a handsome, though quick-tempered young fellow, possessed of a jealous, passionate nature. Philip married a beautiful girl, who was a born coquette.

One night they gave a grand ball, at which the beautiful inconstant young wife flirted outrageously. When the ball was over and all the guests had departed, the young husband called his wife to task about her scandalous conduct. Hot, bitter words ensued, whereupon Philip snatched his father's sword from off the wall and plunged it through his wife's heart. With an agonizing shriek she fell across the bed, her life's blood dyeing her white ball gown and the canopied bed as she fell.

When the young husband realised what he had done, he ran from the room screaming, "I have killed Pauline, my beautiful wife." He still carried the sword in his hand, and just as he reached the entrance doors he stumbled and fell upon it, which, being still wet with the life blood of his wife, pierced his heart.

They buried the couple in the family vault and closed

the old place up. No one has ever lived there since, and the superstitious and weak-minded declared that the place was haunted. Some had even gone so far as to declare that every night at about midnight one could hear the piercing shriek of a woman, then a little while after that, the agonized groan of a man's voice, a dull thud and then the hurrying of many feet and much lamenting, until after a while all sounds would die away and a ghostly silence reign.

This had caused no little terror among the Negroes and poor white people down in the village, and at night it was absolutely impossible to induce the weak-minded ones to traverse the road which led past the Towers.

Richard Vanbrugh had heard this same legend, and it had strengthened his decision of having Florence brought there, for any noise they would cause would only make the Negroes take good care to avoid the place.

In the meantime, the pleasures and amusements at Grey's Villa continued to flow incessantly. Tonight one of the grandest lawn parties of the season would take place. Everything the Greys did was in proper style and of the first class.

Her lawn was decked beautifully to suit the occasion. Rows of quaint Chinese lanterns were swung overhead, and comfortable rustic seats and small tables were placed here and there throughout the spacious lawn.

At one end of the lawn a grand dancing pavilion was erected and decked with trailing evergreens and huge tropical plants. Here the lights were more brilliant than the dull red glare of the lanterns, for in some unique way an arch of brilliant lights was stationed just above the heads of the orchestra.

I have previously said that Florence was lovely, but tonight she seemed peerless in her strange young beauty.

Her mass of brilliant black hair was coiled and pinned in a loose knot at the back of her queenly head, and her graceful figure was set off to advantage by a gown of rich black lace and flashing jet, from the low-cut bodice of which rose her gleaming white shoulders and swan-like throat in charming loveliness.

The women envied her her beautiful face and queen-like carriage, while not a few of the men adored — worshipped the ground she trod upon.

Among the latter, Jack Warrington could be classed, for he was her constant shadow, her most ardent admirer, and Florence looked upon him with no little favor.

He was a tall, light fellow, with large grey eyes and curling black hair, and many were the admiring glances bestowed upon his graceful person as he moved through the crowd in search of the girl of his heart, with whom he was to dance the next dance.

"This is our next dance, Miss Grey," he whispered, when he had found her.

"Yes, I know, I had not forgotten," she answered, with one of her sweetest smiles.

The next moment his arm was around her waist and they were slowly whirling away amid the crowd. For the moment he forgot all — everything, in the joy of being near, touching the girl he loved with all the intensity of his passionate soul. And when it was over, he led her out on the lawn in one of the most secluded spots so as to tell her of his love. It mastered, overpowered him so that he could contain himself no longer.

"Miss Grey — Florence," he began, his voice trembling with passion. "I have brought you here, away from all the crowd to tell you that I love you. Yes, I love you, Florence. I have loved you since the day I first met you. Won't you be my wife, dearest Florence?"

He waited until the silence proved unbearable, and he felt that he must get her to raise her eyes to his at any cost.

"Wait, darling. I have frightened you. I was too abrupt and you are angry with me, but oh Florence, the joy of having you all to myself overpowered me. Something within me, my heart, whispered the words 'I love you'. And I cannot still its mad beating. Won't you come to my arms, dear Florence? Won't you rest your beautiful head upon my heart and whisper to me that you love me?" With one hand he raised her beautiful face to his, while the other went gently around her waist. "Ah, you do love me, Florence. I can see it in your eyes. Speak to me, dear one."

For a moment her beautiful dark eyes gazed into his passionate orbs, then her head fell upon his breast, but not before he caught the faint whisper, "Ah, Jack, my Jack, how I do love you." And he drew her close to him in a passionate embrace and spent his kisses upon her upturned face, and called her his sweetheart, pet, and lastly his dear wife.

Florence was the first to awake from this beautiful dream and with a little cry she whispered, "Oh, Jack, it is late. We must join the others now."

"No, no, dearest, let me have you a little while longer; let's see, we are to dance the next together, and it is just beginning. We will sit it out. But you must be chilly; wait here a moment while I go and get you a shawl."

After giving her another passionate embrace, he left her with the words: "I won't be gone long."

Florence lay back in her seat and closed her eyes so that her dream of love would appear more vivid. She wondered if there was another girl in all the world so happy as she, wondering if there was any other as loving and handsome as her Jack.

Suddenly she heard a slight noise, and slowly unclosing her eyes she turned her head to look; seeing nothing, she lay back again. In another moment she felt a hot breath close to her ear, and with a little cry, she started to her feet, at the same time she was caught in the strong embrace of a man who held a drugged kerchief to her nostrils. She tried to scream to call Jack but the words died on her lips; she gave a piteous moan, a suffocating gasp, and sank into unconsciousness.

Dick Vanbrugh was restlessly pacing the white sandy

road which lay before the Haunted Towers. His covered
carriage stood a little distance from the roadway,
beneath the dense shadows of the overhanging trees,
through the interstices of which the moon gleamed like
long slits of pale silver. There was an air of discontent
about him as with both hands thrust into his trousers
pockets and a frown on his handsome brow he would
pause in the midst of his restless pacing and gaze
expectantly into the distance.

He pulled out his watch and saw by the light of the
pale, round moon overhead that it was 12:30 o'clock.

"I wonder what makes that confounded Negro so
late?" he murmured to himself. "We will barely have
time to reach Lesterville if he doesn't show up soon. Ah,
there he is now," he exclaimed, as the form of Long Tom
appeared in the middle of the road, with the girl
Florence slung over his shoulder.

He withdrew behind the safe shadow of his carriage
as Tom, struggling bravely on, drew nearer.

The rough jolting, together with the cool, refreshing
night breeze had helped to revive the girl, who was now
moaning piteously and struggling to free herself from
the man's embrace. Her brain was clouded. She could
remember nothing distinctly, but she did remember the
party, the dance, and afterwards Jack's dear arms about
her and his passionate love words in her ear. And then
Jack left her — the strange noise, and, oh, God, that
man.

"Help, oh help," she cried, fighting desperately to
free herself. At the same time Vanbrugh rushed up,

pretended to knock Long Tom down and received the
girl, who had now fainted, in his arms. For a moment he
held her passionately to his heart.

"Ah, dear heaven, this one passionate embrace
repays me for all that I have suffered. I would brave the
world for her dear sake," he murmured fervently.

Long Tom had already clambered up to the
coachman's seat, and had driven the horses around so
that the carriage now stood in the road.

But just at this time the girl regained her senses, and
with a faint cry, she staggered to her feet.

"Jack! Oh, where am I?" she cried, gazing
bewilderedly about her.

"Pardon me, miss, but an attempted insult has been
played upon you, I fear; and I am indeed glad that I was
near enough to render you my assistance," said
Vanbrugh, in his most charming and gallant manner.

"Oh, thank you so much, sir, but you will not leave
me. I — oh, my brain is so confused — but you will not
let him touch me, sir?" she cried, piteously.

"Have no fear of that, miss. I will drive you home in
my carriage if you will allow me that honor."

"Then you know who I am, sir?" she asked, trying to
get a glimpse of his face. But that crafty gentleman kept
his face averted.

"Pardon me, my dear young lady, but I think
everyone about the country here knows who Miss
Florence Grey is," he answered, at the same time
assisting her into the carriage. Then, jumping in himself,
he closed the door, and the vehicle rumbled quietly,

though with great speed, down the road. And Vanbrugh with a triumphant expression in his eyes, settled himself back in the dense shadow of the carriage.

Florence's brain was, by this time, growing clearer, and as she looked out the carriage window, she saw that the carriage was taking her from, instead of to, her home. With a faint cry, she turned to Vanbrugh, but a turn in the road had thrown the moonlight full upon his face, and she saw before her the man who had several times attempted a flirtation with her. Involuntarily, she started to her feet with an expression of indignation stamped upon her every feature.

"Sir! What does this mean?" she demanded.

"It means, dearest Florence, that I love you and want you to be my wife. I love you, Florence. I have loved you since the day I first saw you. Forgive me, my darling, but when I first beheld your beautiful face, I swore then that I would make you my beloved mistress, but when I attempted to flirt with you I saw that I could only win you by making you my wife. As I also saw that it was impossible to make you my wife until I had you in my power, I concluded to have you abducted so that I would have a chance to win your love. Be mine, dear Florence, and you shall have servants by the score. I will take you abroad, where the difference of color will not be questioned. You shall live in a palace amid a grove of orange trees, and with spacious balconies leading down to a bay as blue as the heavens above. Darling of my heart, if you will."

During this passionate love avowal, the girl had

remained standing with features as white and as immovable as a marble statue. And no pen could describe the expression of scorn and contempt that flashed from her beautiful eyes. And when he fell on his knees before her and attempted to catch her beautiful hands in his, she drew back with a scornful gesture and hissed:

"Wretch. Do not dare to touch me. I despise you. Let me out at once, or I shall scream for help."

Dick Vanbrugh was confounded. That this colored girl had refused his offer of love and marriage, he, the Hon. Richard Vanbrugh, who could with very little effort marry of the first society, astounded, dazed him.

"Florence," he said, trying to gain one of her hands.

"Wretch! Do not dare to touch me. Stand aside, or else open this door and let me pass out of your hated presence."

Vanbrugh had not dreamed that this beautiful creature was possessed of so much spirit. Her words stung, maddened him, while her beauty set his soul on fire; but with a great effort he calmed himself, and his voice was quite calm when next he addressed her.

"My dear Florence, calm yourself, for when you leave this carriage you will be either my promised wife or my prisoner. Why not be reasonable and leave it as my adored one?"

"Coward! Wretch! I would die first. I tell you I will never marry you. Never. For I hate you. Let me out or I shall scream for help."

"That would be very foolish, as well as quite useless,

for we are far beyond all hearing distance. Be seated, loved one or I am afraid you will be quite exhausted by the time we reach our destination."

"Oh, God, what would you do? Surely, you would not take me away against my will. Ah, you could not be so heartless."

"Heartless. Oh, my love, it is you who are heartless. I love you with the intensity of my soul. I love you better than my honor, better than my life," he exclaimed, with a passion that shook his whole person. Florence caught a glimpse of his passionate face, and, dastard that he was, a little pity stole into her heart for him; but remembering the cowardly trick he had played upon her, her hatred crushed it out.

"Why can you not love or even pity me, Florence? I have suffered tortures since I first gazed upon your fatal beauty. But if you give me one good reason why you do not love me, God, how it pains me to say it, I will let you go."

"I cannot love you, sir," replied Florence as gently as she could, "because I love another, and even if I did not, I don't think that I could ever love you."

A jealous pang smote his heart, and with a smothered oath he hissed, his hot breath falling with fearful force on her neck.

"By heavens! No. I yield thee to no man. And by fair or foul means, I shall make you my wife."

Thinking of the loving mother, devoted lover, and all of her dear friends and companions, the beautiful girl fell on her knees before him.

"Oh, sir, see, I kneel, I pray, I entreat you to let me go. If there is one spark of manly feeling within your breast let me go to those I love and who love me. If I should give my consent to marry you, no good would result from such an unholy union."

How beautiful she looked. On her pale, upturned face he could not see the misery, he only saw her beauty which fascinated, stole his senses from him. He could scarcely control the impulse to clasp her to his heart, to kiss rapturously the soft, scarlet lips.

"My God, Florence, I would be mad to give you up. No I cannot, by heavens, I will not let you go. For I love you — you are dearer to me than heaven itself."

"Oh, God," she cried, rising slowly to her feet, "is there indeed no hope, no chance of escape from this villain whom I hate with all the intensity of my soul." Then turning her white, set face to him, she said, "Coward! I see there is no chance of escape, but my friends will some day come to my rescue, though if they should fail to find me, I shall never give up hope until my hair is gray and my back bent double, and death is staring me in the face. Now, do your worst, for I will never, never, change my decision."

"We shall see, my fair one," he answered, and the girl, not even glancing at him, seated herself in the corner of the vehicle and gazed out of the window.

During this time the carriage had been speeding rapidly along the highway, and in two hours' time it stopped before the tall entrance gate of a beautiful, vine-clad villa.

Dick opened the door, alighted, and held out his hand to assist Florence, saying, "Welcome to Lesterville, your future home, my darling. Though this is but a playhouse to what I would give you if you would only say the word."

Florence answered him with not so much as a look, but sprung past his hand to the ground. It was chilly in the early morning atmosphere, and being clad in her low-cut evening gown, she shuddered slightly.

"What a brute I am," said Dick, and feeling in the carriage he drew forth a dark, though lightweight wrap and threw it about her shoulders as they proceeded towards the house. With a latchkey he noiselessly opened the door. At the same time a fat, black, middle aged woman emerged from a doorway and approached them with loud and hearty exclamations.

"Lord, is that you, Mr. Richard? None of the other servants is up yet. I hope you don't mind, sah, 'cause it's jest little after five o'clock. Lord, is this Miss Kate? Poor thing, she 'pears kinda tired."

"Yes, mammy, this is the much talked of Miss Kate. Show her to her room now. This long journey has fatigued both of us considerably."

"My poor boy, 'deed honey, just you go to you own room, and after I show Miss Kate hers, I'll make both of you a strong cup of coffee."

This short dialogue did not surprise Florence. Indeed, she was prepared for anything that might happen, for what dastard trick was this villain not capable of? But come what may, she would put her faith and trust in the One who always looks down upon His little ones when they are in need.

It took Jack Warrington quite a little while to find a wrap to put about his loved one's shoulders, and when he did find it he hastened to take it to her, but upon reaching the spot where he had left her, she was not there.

"Perhaps," he told himself, "some of the girls have carried her off; anyway I shall ask Miss Payne."

Sadie was seated in the midst of a crowd of young men, flirting, as James always said, "to beat the band."

"I beg your pardon, Miss Payne, but have you seen Miss Grey?"

"Did I see Miss Grey? Dear me, when and how did you lose her?" she asked in mock surprise, and a mischievous twinkle in her bewitching eyes.

"My dear Jack, don't mind Sadie. She always pokes fun at everybody. Come and sit by me and join in this little discussion we are having, for I dare say Florrie will turn up pretty soon," put in James laughingly.

And not wishing to appear too disconcerted, Jack was forced to join in the merriment which was always sure to be found around the witty Sadie.

But as the time sped on and Florence failed to put in an appearance, James as well as Jack grew anxious, and went in search of her. By this time two or three other girls, missing the sweet face, had also joined in the search. A servant was called and sent to the villa in search of her, but after a short while returned with the reply that Miss Florrie was not in the house.

"Nonsense," cried Mrs. Grey, trying to speak naturally, "Miss Florence must be in her room," and she hastily left the crowd, and went in search of Florence, herself.

But she returned quite hastily, and with much consternation, saying that she could not find the dear child anywhere, and wondering what possessed her to play so cruel a trick upon them. It was not like Florence to act so strangely.

By this time the dancing and gaieties had abruptly come to a halt, and even the musicians joined in the search for the missing girl.

Jack Warrington hastened to the little rustic seat in which he had left his darling, the crowd following closely. He was telling them why he left her there, when someone picked up a dainty bit of white lace and a few trampled roses.

"Good God, what does this mean?" exclaimed Jack, in an agonized voice as he stared at the articles just mentioned.

"What, oh, what is it?" asked Mrs. Grey, distractedly rushing up. "My heavens, they are the roses my darling carried in her hand, and that is her kerchief. Oh, God, what has happened to my dear one?"

Just then someone exclaimed, "Here is her fan," and another, "Here are the roses and the much admired pearl headed pin she wore in her hair."

And for a while consternation and distraction

reigned supreme.

What followed can better be described by the insertion of a couple of extracts from the Washington newspapers:

NEGRO HEIRESS KIDNAPPED

Miss Florence Grey, the daughter of a respectable and well-bred mulattress, has suddenly disappeared, and it is supposed that the young woman, who is a very beautiful octoroon, has been kidnapped. The Greys are very wealthy, and were staying at Grey's Villa, their summer residence, situated about twenty miles from Washington on the Virginia side. A garden or lawn festival was in progress at the time of the supposed abduction, which was brought to quite an abrupt and distracting termination, for the young woman was very highly esteemed by her own people and not a few of the whites.

'From an Afra-American news edition.'
THE ABDUCTION OF MISS FLORENCE GREY
OUR BEAUTIFUL SOCIETY BELLE

Miss Florence Grey, our beautiful and accomplished society leader, has it is feared, been abducted from Grey's Villa, their magnificent country place.

Mrs. Estelle Grey, the young lady's widowed mother, and Dr. James Grey, her brother, are quite prostrated over this most unfortunate piece of ill-luck, and have offered a reward of $500.00 for information of the whereabouts of the young lady.

*A unique lawn party was going on at the time of this
startling disappearance, which was brought abruptly and
unceremoniously to an end, while all — even the musicians
themselves, joined in the search for the missing girl, who is a
great favorite with all who know her.*

*Special detectives, William Wright and Henry K. Miller,
have been despatched from this city, and are doing all in their
power to find the missing one. Mr. John Warrington of the
well-known firm of Warrington and Carland of Boston, was
one of the young lady's most ardent admirers, and was in her
company a short time before her disappearance. He is quite
distracted, and is working like a hero to bring to light the
mystery of this strange disappearance.*

"You, Susan. You Jinnie, you gals better get up and
come downstairs. It's almost five o'clock. Miss Kate and
Mr. Richard done already come and you all laying in
bed like it was night. 'Deed you better come down here
at once," screamed the voice of mammy, the black
woman, after she had shown Florence to her room, and
was bustling about the kitchen, preparing 'Mr. Richard
and Miss Kate' a dainty luncheon. In a short time, two
girls entered the kitchen, and with a quiet "Good
morning, Aunt Amy," proceeded to busy themselves
with sundry duties.

One — the one called Susie — was a tall, dark girl
about twenty years of age, and possessing a pleasing
and quiet disposition, while the other was short, stout,
and rather light complexioned with a jovial, fun-loving

disposition, and was always getting herself into mischief by, as her aunt always said " 'tending to other folks' 'fairs."

"You said Mr. Vanbrugh and his cousin had arrived, Aunt Amy?" she asked, with much curiosity.

"Yes," replied her aunt.

"What an unusual hour for folks to arrive from an institution? Don't you think it seems strange?"

"That's Mr. Richard's business," replied her aunt, rather sharply. "I tells you 'bout niggers, they never will have nothing or be nothing nohow. Why? 'Cause every last one of 'em is too meddlesome," and with her head well up in the air, and the tray of dainties in her hands, she indignantly left the kitchen.

She carried the tray to Dick's room first, and arranged daintily on a little table a plate of cold chicken, some home-made bread, fresh butter, a small pot of steaming, fragrant coffee and a pitcher of cream.

Vanbrugh thanked her, telling her that it seemed like old times to have her fixing things for him in such a motherly way, but that she had better take Miss Kate hers before the coffee got cold, cautioning her to answer no questions Miss Kate might see fit to ask, but to leave her to herself, until after she had rested, when by that time she would probably be all right. But on no account must she leave her mistress' door unlocked.

The woman, whom we shall hereafter call mammy, unlocked the door of Florence's sitting room, entered, arranged the contents of the tray on a small table and left the apartment, locking it after her.

The room was a large, well-ventilated sitting room, opening into a dainty bedroom beyond. The floor was of polished hardwood, in the centre of which was spread a rich Turkish rug, while some exceedingly comfortable chairs and a fine leather couch were arranged around with very good taste. A few good water colors decked the walls and cool, dainty curtains of the finest Swiss hung from the long bay windows.

When mammy entered, Florence had the windows hoisted and was searching about the room for some means of escape.

"Here, honey, come 'long, eat your vittles 'fore your coffee gits cold," She said, at the same time spreading the dainty repast on a small table.

Florence did not so much as glance in her direction, and the woman, murmuring, "Poor thing," left the room, not forgetting to lock the door after her.

After mammy was gone, Florence searched in vain for some means of escape, but her efforts were soon exhausted and with a wild, heart-rending cry, she threw herself down upon the leather couch. It was some moments afterwards that she heard the grating of a key in the door, and with a cry of alarm she started to her feet and found herself face to face with Vanbrugh.

"You — why are you here? Can you not leave me to myself for even a few moments?" she asked.

"So this is how you repay me for my love and gentle kindness, is it, Florence? Why do you compel me to speak harshly to you? Why not be reasonable and come to my arms as my adored one?"

"You forget," she said with icy coldness, "that I love and am beloved by one of my own race."

"It is you who must forget that, Florence," said Vanbrugh, impatiently. "You are mine — I yield you to no man. You shall never even see him again."

"Oh, misery," exclaimed she, burying her face in both hands.

Vanbrugh pushed a chair toward her, and she sunk into it, removing as with an effort, her hands from her face. Whatever struggle she had undergone was now passed, and her face was as calm, as white as a statue.

"Listen to me, Florence. You are in my power, and by lowering myself to the standard of a brute, I could force you submit to anything that I might desire. It is in my power to ruin your character — to bring your proud spirit to the dust. I offered you my heart and hand, and with insolence you hurled them back into my face. Although I love you still, that insult I shall never forget. I do not desire to marry you now, but I shall force you to live with me as my mistress, and when I am tired of you, when your character is spoiled and your beauty faded, you may go back to your lover and receive the insults you hurled at me."

He stopped to see what effect his words carried, but her face wore an expression of mingled scorn and loathing that the meanest hound would have slunk from.

"I thought you a villain, but I had yet to learn what deeds of infamy you were capable of. I do not fear you, for if the worst comes I can but die. And I will die by my own hand before I submit to your brutish, degrading desires. But I will not die without a struggle. As heartless as your servants may be, I will appeal to them, for there may be one who still retains a spark of pity and would not stop to hesitate if one of their own race was in trouble."

"These servants as well as yourself are in my power. Listen, there is yet something else to learn. You are only fifteen miles from Grey's Villa, and yet no help will ever come to you. Your friends and associates, being only Negroes, would not dare to think of searching for you in the home of the Hon. Richard Vanbrugh, and even if they did, they would not know that I am staying at Lesterville until after my desires have been fulfilled.

"These servants here think that you are an insane cousin of mine, who went mad some years ago. They think that I have brought you here to try and recall your mind by bright, new scenes and my handsome person which you went mad over. Scream then, and they will pay no heed to your cries. Neither will anyone else hear you, for few pass this way and there is not another villa within a mile of Lesterville. Therefore, you are in my power and must — will be forced to accede to my wishes."

"Villain, you have planned it well, but advance one step nearer me and I will bury this dagger in my heart, and you shall be held accountable for my murder."

So saying, her small, white hand drew from the bosom of her black lace dress a jewelled dagger.

"Stay your hand, my beauty, I will give you three

days to think the matter over, at the end of which time I shall come for my reward."

And he left her as softly as he had approached her.

The moment the door closed upon him, Florence began to tremble with anguish and fear.

"If I remain in this house, I am utterly in the power of this wretch. He has the key of my apartments in his possession. At the end of three days he said he would come again. He will force me to listen to his infamous proposals unless I — oh, God, it is terrible, terrible. Oh, Jack, Jack, could you only know what agony I am suffering. To die alone — oh, my heavens. Oh, merciful Father," sobbed the girl in the anguish of her soul. So bitter was her grief that she had not heard the door open and a woman enter.

"Lord, honey, what's the matter? Poor Miss Kate, come to your ole mammy nurse, honey," said mammy, for it was she who had entered, with genuine affection.

"My good woman, you will help me. You will have pity and help me to escape from this wretched place. See, I beg you to help me, on my bended knees. This man, Mr. Vanbrugh, has deceived you. I am not his cousin Kate as he made you believe."

"Lord, chile, 'deed you is Miss Kate. You is her very image; you has the same hair, the same eyes and they are just as wild as they was when you was took away from here five years ago. So if you ain't Miss Kate, then who is you?"

"Oh, God, how can I make you understand. I am Florence Grey, a colored girl."

" 'Deed you ain't no colored gal, chile. Lordy, lemme get outta here, 'cause I believe you done gone clean, spank crazy."

And mammy, with genuine fright, backed out of the apartment, slammed and locked the door, and with quick footsteps sought Vanbrugh, telling that gentleman that indeed she was afraid of Miss Kate, and it was her opinion that Mr. Richard better take her back to the institution where she come from, adding that if he didn't take her back he'd have to send Susan to wait on her.

"Why, what is the matter? What has Miss Kate been doing?" asked Vanbrugh.

"Doing? Good Lord, she is carrying on very awful, indeed. Why, bless yo' soul, chile, she nearly tore all my clothes off, begging me to save her and glaring about all excited like."

The situation was so ludicrous that Vanbrugh burst into a hearty laugh; and mammy, with a "Good Lord, what you see to laugh at?" indignantly flounced out of the room.

To hear that mammy was afraid of Florence was just exactly what Vanbrugh wanted. It would save him much trouble while at the same time it would place that arrogant woman more firmly in his power. He rung the bell and asked Jennie, who answered it, to send Susie to him.

"Mammy tells me that she is afraid of Miss Kate, do you think that you could take mammy's place as waiting maid?" he asked, as Susie quietly entered the room.

"Yes, sir, I can," answered she, with quiet respect.

"Knowing that Miss Kate is a harmless imbecile, I don't think you would be easily frightened by any of her strange actions, would you?"

"No, oh no, sir."

"You are a good, sensible girl," answered Vanbrugh significantly, "and if you attend to your duties well, you shall be liberally rewarded. You may go now, but, one thing more, will you try to get that tiny dagger from her, and keep all dangerous weapons out of her reach? For I am afraid she might try to do herself bodily harm," and he handed the girl a silver coin, after which she thanked him, bowed respectfully, and withdrew.

Some moments afterwards she made Jennie, who, if she was a meddlesome Mattie and a chatterbox, could keep a secret, acquainted with the above conversation.

"And another thing, Jennie, I don't believe this young lady is Mr. Vanbrugh's cousin at all."

"Why don't you think so, Susie?"

"I have my own reasons, as well as suspicions, and I will tell you exactly what I mean before the day is gone."

And do what she might, Jennie could get nothing more from the quiet Susie.

But to return to Florence — she had composed herself somewhat, and was seated in a rocker trying to interest herself in a book which she had picked up from the table. She had prayed to God and pleaded to humanity and both had turned a deaf ear. So, after all, she thought, though not without a degree of sadness, if the worst came, she could but die. How glad she was that she had her tiny, jewelled dagger in her possession. She had playfully placed it in her bosom last night while she was dressing for the lawn fete, and one of her girlfriends had remarked that she looked like a Spanish princess and another had picked up the tiny weapon and placed it in the folds of black lace, saying: "Now in truth you are a princess, for you have your jewels, dagger, and around you are gathered your pleading subjects and many gallant knights." During the fun and laughter that had ensued, she had forgotten to take the dagger out.

Oh, how happy she was then. Why, it was only last night; but to the unhappy girl it seemed that days, weeks had passed since Jack Warrington had clasped her in his strong arms and, whispering words of love and devotion, tenderly asked her to be his wife.

The grating of the key in the door harshly interrupted her. Good heavens, had that wretch come back to torment her again? Could he not leave her alone for even one hour? No, it was not Vanbrugh, it was only the woman with the tray — her dinner perhaps. But this was a new face, not that of the horrid old woman, but the kind, sympathetic face of a young girl, and Florence wondered if this girl possessed a heart as kind and as sympathetic as was the dark though comely face.

Susie — for it was she — set the tray on a table and looked up to encounter two beautiful, sad eyes gazing appealingly at her. She started suddenly and with an expression of infinite surprise, stared hard at Florence.

'She also thinks me mad, and is afraid of me', thought Florence, while Susie was mentally exclaiming 'I have seen that face before. Ah, she is — I cannot be mistaken — Florence Grey! She is certainly Florence Grey'.

"What is the matter? Do I frighten you also, girl?"

"No, oh no, you do not frighten me, but I have seen your face before. You are Florence Grey, a girl of color," cried Susie excitedly.

With a glad cry, Florence fell upon her knees at the girl's feet.

"Oh, God of mercy. You are right. I am Florence Grey, and in the power of this wretch. But yours is a kind face — you will not turn from me. You will help me to escape from here?" she cried, frantically.

"With all my heart. But rise and calm yourself, we must not be overheard," said Susie, who had now regained her usual quiet manner.

And Florence arose, and leading Susie into the dainty bedroom where they were not likely to be overheard, related to her her pitiful story, ending with, "And you will help me? May God bless you, but you must have heard that I was very wealthy — and I will reward you liberally — richly if you will only help me to escape, for I fear I should indeed have gone mad if I remained here many more hours."

"Say no more, Miss Florence. My sister and I will do all in our power to help you. As for Aunt Amy, she is the kindest person I know, but being very ignorant, and Mr.

Vanbrugh's nurse since the villain was an infant in long clothes, she would place his word above all else."

And after telling Florence that she would come in again later in the afternoon to make some plan of escape, adding that it looked suspicious for her to remain with her too long, she left the apartment.

Susie and Jennie Hill were orphans, whose parents had died within the same week of that dread disease, yellow fever. Both girls were attending the industrial institution at Hampton, Va., at the time, and as can be imagined, the death of both of their parents at the same time, was a sore trial to the young girls; for Susie was just sixteen and Jennie fourteen and they were left penniless, as well as friendless, except for an aunt, who, as Susie has already said, was very kind to them.

The education of these two girls was brought to an abrupt, cruel ending, and with as much heart as they had left they were forced to seek employment in Washington, the home of employment. Mammy procured situations for them in the home of first class people and none of your poor white trash, in which homes the girls had remained until Dick Vanbrugh returned from abroad and made his plans known to mammy.

His plans were as follows:

Mammy was to procure two other servants, friends of hers, if possible, and go down to Lesterville, one of his smallest country villas, and make ready to receive him and his cousin Kate, who had lost her reason five years ago, but whom he was going to take to the country to try to restore her reason by new scenery, fresh air, and his own presence. Susie had often heard her aunt talking about this cousin, how, in mammy's own words, "Mr. Richard wouldn't marry her and the poor thing took it to heart so that she run clean crazy, and Mr. Richard took her to a private institution. But 'deed, chile, Mr. Richard was mighty sorry for poor Miss Kate, so shutting the house up and paying for my board until he come back he went to some place or another, I dunno where. That was five years ago, and when he come home again and tells me to go down to Lesterville and fix up things for he and Miss Kate, I was most filled with joy, bless his dear heart."

Mammy did not know that this same beautiful Miss Kate had died two years after being placed in the institution.

Jennie's curiosity had been aroused to such a high pitch by this piece of news that she had not formed any opinion whatever as to the truth of Vanbrugh's plan, but Susie, on the contrary, thought deeply, telling herself that as wild a life as Mr. Vanbrugh had led, it was not at all likely that he would take an insane cousin, whom he had treated so cruelly, out of an institution and sacrifice his pleasures for so vain an attempt as that. 'Good gracious, who can be silly enough to believe such an absurd story'? she asked herself. But then, Mr. Vanbrugh would reward them handsomely for their services, and besides if there was very much villainy attached to it, who knew but what she and Jennie might not gain enough by their faithful services to help repair their interrupted education. She only needed two more years' study before she would graduate, and Jennie — poor, dear Jennie — did so long to be a school teacher.

So they had come to Lesterville, and she, Susie, had found out that it was just as she had suspected. Richard Vanbrugh was still at his old tricks. And this time he had in his power the beautiful Florence Grey, a famous and well-loved girl who had shown so brightly in last season's world of fashion. Try to compel her — oh, the wretch. But even if Florence was only a pauper, she would run the chance of losing anything Vanbrugh might have given them by saving this sweet and beautiful young girl.

So she and Jennie quietly let themselves out of the house that evening about nine o'clock with fleeting footsteps guided by human sympathy, and a brief instruction from Florence.

It was a beautiful night. The moon was just rising, and myriads of stars peeped forth from the cloudless blue heavens peeping through the branches of the tall, wide spreading trees which nearly met over the broad highway, down which the two girls who, with a prayer on their lips sped onward like two angels of mercy.

"Oh, I hope we won't be missed," exclaimed Jennie.

"No danger of that until tomorrow morning, the thing to hope is that we may reach Grey's Villa before morning. If we don't, I fear for the worst," answered Susie, as she quickened her footsteps.

"We ought to reach there before morning; fifteen miles are not so many. Why, Sue, dear, we have often walked that distance in five hours."

"Yes, I know that Jennie; but as we do not know the exact route, we may strike out on the wrong path and are liable to walk twice fifteen miles before we are through."

"Oh, God help us, I hope not."

"So do I. But don't let's talk any more. It's too exhausting.

"My dear Jack, brace up; all hope is not yet lost. Mr. Miller tells me that he hopes to give us news of our lost one in a few hours," said a friend of Jack Warrington's early on the second morning after the abduction.

Jack was unable to sleep, and had come out early, and with this friend he was taking a stroll in the early morning air to try and quiet his nerves, which had been on the verge of mania ever since that fatal night. Presently they came upon Dr. Grey who was standing against a tree, smoking a cigar and, it seemed, trying to compose his mind.

The others stopped, and all three engaged in an earnest conversation which they had carried on for about five minutes when somebody touched Jack's arm.

All three turned to look and saw two dust laden, excited young ladies.

"Pardon me, sirs, but would you kindly tell us if we are far from Grey's Villa?" asked Susie.

"Why, this is Grey's Villa," answered Jack, staring at them in wonderment.

"Then, oh, thank God, we have found her friends. You sir, must be Miss Florence Grey's brother," exclaimed Susie, pointing at James.

And before anyone else could speak Jennie exclaimed excitedly, "We have just left Miss Grey. She is in great trouble in the power of an unscrupulous white man, and if you don't make haste you will be too late to save her."

"Oh, my God, do you hear, Jim. Oh, speak girl, tell us where she is that I can find my darling," cried Jack.

Susie was quietly telling Dr. Grey the particulars, adding that he must procure the best horses he could find in order to reach Lesterville in time.

As will be imagined, the greatest excitement ensued for about ten minutes, at the end of which time a carriage with a smart lad in the coachman's seat, and Susie, Dr. Grey and John Warrington on the inside, tore madly down the road.

As it tore through the streets of the village, the well-shod feet of the thoroughbreds made such a noise that all who heard it ran to the doors, window, gates or whichever place was nearest, exclaiming:

"A runaway horse."

"Good Lord, it's Grey's carriage."

"I wonder what's up now!"

Jennie had remained behind so as to break the news to Mrs. Grey, that lady receiving her in her arms as she would have received one of her most intimate friends, commanding the servants to bring the lady some refreshments, while with her own delicate hands she relieved Jennie of her dust laden garments, and on the whole, making her as comfortable as possible.

The news had spread rapidly. One of the servants from Grey's Villa had run down to the village and told one family of Negroes, and in a few moments great crowds of men women and children were gathered together in groups, in their houses, yards, pavements and even in the road conversing, some loudly and vulgarly, others in excited whispers.

Some were saying that "Florence wasn't kidnapped no way, but had run off with a white man," others that "I'd like to receive that reward them two gals would get," "Wonder what time they'll get back," "I'm just dying to see Miss Florence just to see how she looks," "Spects she'll turn her nose up a us now and hole her head higher than ever," and other remarks too vulgar to repeat.

The reader perhaps would like to know what has become of Long Tom. That gentleman, after driving Vanbrugh and Florence to Lesterville, unharnessed and stabled the horse and, after receiving $500 in small bank notes to avoid suspicion, walked to the nearest station, and boarding a train he left for Washington. And, Negro like, after making a loud display, left for a Northern city. It is well to add also that he was killed — cut to death in a gambling affray some years later.

"You Susan! You Jinnie! You all better come downstairs! Here 'tis most seven o'clock and not one of you up yet. I bound if I comes up there you'll come down quick enuff!" exclaimed mammy, in her usual loud voice.

"Confound it! Will she never stop yelling! How in thunder is a fellow going to sleep!" Vanbrugh got up, threw on his dressing robe and rung the bell angrily.

"Mammy, what the devil is the matter with you this morning? I want you to shut up that noise yelling after those accursed girls, and let me sleep!" he exclaimed angrily, as mammy answered the ring.

"Lord bless yo' soul, Mr. Richard, I can't get them children up this morning to save my life."

"Then go up and pitch them down; I don't care if you break their necks. Anyway, don't let me hear any more of that infernal yelling!" and with this savage response he slammed the door, leaving that good old soul standing staring at the panels of the latter object and wondering to herself what had come over Mr. Richard.

Meanwhile, all the sleep having left Vanbrugh's eyes by this time, he began to slowly make his toilet, but was startlingly interrupted in a very few moments by mammy, who was knocking on his door and exclaiming that "Susan and Jinnie can't be found nowhere!" and that "Miss Kate's door was locked from the inside."

"The devil!" exclaimed Vanbrugh impatiently, "I'll be there directly, mammy. Meanwhile, search the park and neighboring woods."

He was interrupted by mammy's voice saying that the big gates were open and two white gentlemen were driving up in a buggy.

Vanbrugh finished his toilet quick enough now, and was on the verandah just in time to receive the two gentlemen who had alighted and were ascending the steps.

"Good morning, sir. Mr. Vanbrugh, I presume," said one of the men. They were detectives Wright and Miller.

Vanbrugh bowed gallantly, saying in his cold, well-bred manner, "Yes, I have the honor of bearing that title. What can I do for you?"

"We, sir, are detectives Wm. Wright and Mr. Miller; we are searching for a young lady by the name of Miss Florence Grey."

Another interruption. This time it was the approach of a carriage drawn by a pair of wild horses which came dashing up the wide graveled drive and pulled up before them. Almost before the carriage had stopped, the door was thrown wide and two young men alighted.

"By George, what does this mean!" exclaimed both detectives at the same time.

"Florence — my darling — have you found her?" cried both men simultaneously.

"I beg your pardon, my friends, what does this abrupt intrusion mean?" asked Vanbrugh in his cool and most scornful manner.

"Villain! Wretch! I tell you, Mr. Miller, she is in this house, suffering — perhaps dead!"

"This girl whom you seek, Florence Grey, is my mistress!" exclaimed Vanbrugh, insolently.

"You lie!" exclaimed James and Jack as with one breath.

"How dare you, you impudent Negro!" and Vanbrugh drew a revolver and aimed it at Jack's head, but with a lightning quickness, that young man knocked his hand back with such force that the weapon went off, the discharge passing through Vanbrugh's brain and he fell dead.

Meanwhile, Susie had alighted from the carriage by the other door and unperceived by the men, had entered a side door which led directly to Florence's apartments, and with "It's I, Miss Florence; all's well, let me in," she had explained briefly to Florence what was happening, had descended the stairs and rushed out on the porch just in time to see the revolver discharge.

Both girls gave a piercing shriek as Vanbrugh reeled and fell heavily to the floor.

Jack caught Florence's fainting form in his arms, exclaiming wildly, "Florence, darling, do not faint. It is I, Jack. Good God, Jim, she doesn't know me. Water, girl, quick. She is suffocating. Oh, Florence. Oh, my love, my love."

"Let me have her, Jack; she will be all right presently. She has only fainted, dear precious girl. How glad, how happy mother will be," said Dr. Grey.

The two detectives, unlike men of their profession, were as excited as the rest, while mammy, who had witnessed all, was on her knees crying, "Poor Mr. Richard. Poor Mr. Richard."

A few hours later Florence was gathered lovingly in

a mother's arms, and many were the tears and rejoicings of that happy household.

Being only a girl of color no great stir was made over this awful tragedy, excepting through the newspapers. Those terrible mediums spread the news far and wide, one paper declaring that the beautiful Negress had run off with Richard Vanbrugh of her own free will, and had caused him to commit suicide by deserting him and playing lady when caught up with.

But through it all, Florence lived and shone as conspicuously ever in her world of fashion, which received her with open arms.

A year later she was the blushing bride of Jack Warrington who took her to his Northern home, where Mrs. Grey and James followed her, the latter bringing with him as his bride the winsome Sadie Payne.

Susie and Jennie were liberally rewarded, and with happy hearts and smiling faces they again took up their studies.

One more word. Mammy was mentioned in the Hon. Richard Vanbrugh's will as an old and faithful servant to whom was to be left $5,000, the rest of his large fortune to be divided up between different charitable institutions in case he had no wife.

Mammy was simply delighted, saying that "Mr. Richard always was a good boy, and bless his dear heart, she'd soon join him in heaven."

So with many good wishes and blessings we will leave our dear friends, hoping, as with the ending of a fairy tale, they may live very happily ever afterwards.

THE TEST OF MANHOOD
Sarah A. Allen (Pauline E. Hopkins)

The shed door creaked softly, and Mark Myers stood for a moment peering into the semi-darkness of the twilight. He was a stalwart lad of about eighteen, with soft dark curls, big dark eyes, and the peach-like complexion of a girl, but he was only a Negro, what the colored people designate as "milk and molasses, honey; neither one thing nor the other," and he was leaving his home to try his fortune in the North.

One day Mark had carried a white gentleman's bag to the teamboat landing and as he loitered about the pier after pocketing a generous fee, the words of the patron in conversation with another white man sank in his heart:

"After all this wasted blood and treasure, the Negro question is still uppermost in the South. Why don't you settle it once and for all, Morgan?"

"We might were it not for the infernal interference of

you Yankees, and amalgamation. The mulattoes are the curse of the South. We can't entirely ignore our brothers' cousins and closer kindred, so there you are."

"Your 'brothers and closer kindred' could settle the question themselves if they knew their power."

"How?" queried Morgan.

"Easily enough; when the white blood is pronounced, just disappear and turn up again as a white man. Half of your sectional difficulties would end under such a system."

"And would you, a white man, be willing to encounter the risk that such a course would entail — the wholesale pollution of our race?" thundered the man called Morgan, in disgust.

"Why not? You know the old saying: *Where ignorance is bliss 'tis folly to be wise. Better that than a greater evil.*"

"You Northerners are a riddle."

They passed out of sight and Mark heard no more, but from that time he had thought incessantly of the stranger's words, and at last he resolved to become a white man. And one night when his mother lay peacefully sleeping, with no foreshadowing of the sorrow in store for her, with a backward look of regret and a tear stealing down his cheek, he had stolen softly from the little cabin under the wide spreading magnolia. At the top of the hill he paused for a last look and then turned his face sorrowfully toward the great unknown world, henceforth to be his only home. The day broke; the sun rose; there was a stir of life all about him. How sweet the air smelled; surely there could be no prettier mornings up in the wonderful North to which he was journeying.

As he trudged along with his small bundle over his shoulder he murmured to himself, "Mammy's up now, but she won't miss me yet. I'm glad I chopped all that wood yesterday. It ought to last her a week and better. The white folks all think the world of her. They'll take care of her 'til I get settled; then I'll write and tell her all about my plans."

He avoided the main roads and kept to the fields, thus keeping clear of all chance acquaintances who might interfere with his determination to identify himself with the white race.

The weary time passed on; days were merged into weeks when one morning, tired and fainting with hunger, Mark found himself in the street of a great Northern metropolis, homeless and nearly penniless. He walked through the thoroughfares with the puzzled uncertainty of a stranger doubtful of his route, pausing at intervals to study the signs, feeling his heart sink as he watched the hurrying throng of unfamiliar faces. The scene was so different from his beautiful southern home that in his heart he cried aloud for the dear familiar scenes. Then he remembered and took up his weary tramp again and his search for a friendly face that he might venture to accost the owner for work. Night was approaching and he must have a place to sleep. As he neared the common and its tranquil, inviting greenness burst upon his view, he determined that if nothing better presented itself, to pass the night there under the canopy of heaven.

As he neared Tremont Street a gentleman passed him, evidently in a great hurry; scarcely had his resounding footsteps ceased upon the concrete walk, when Mark noticed a pocket book lying directly at his feet. He picked it up, opened it and saw that it was filled with bills of large denominations. *John E. Brown* was printed in gold letters upon one of the compartments.

Mark stood a second, hesitating as to the right course to pursue. Here was wealth — money for food, shelter, clothes — he sighed as he thought of what it would give him. But only for a moment, the next he was rushing along the wide mall at his utmost speed trying to overtake the gentleman whom he could just discern making his hurried way through the throng of pedestrians.

At the corner of Summer and Washington streets, Mark, breathless and hatless, caught up with the gentleman.

"Eh, what? My pocket book?" ejaculated Mr. Brown, as he felt in all his pockets, and looked down curiously upon the forlorn figure that had tugged so resolutely at his arm to attract his attention.

"Now that was clever of you and very honest, my boy," said the great lawyer, gazing at him over his gold-rimmed spectacles. "Here's something for you," and he placed a bill in the lad's hand that fairly made the dark eyes bulge with surprise. "From the country, aren't you?"

"Yes, suh."

"I thought so. Honesty doesn't flourish in city air. Well I haven't time to talk to you today. Come and see me tomorrow at my office; perhaps I can help you. Want a job don't you?"

"Yes, suh; I'm a stranger in Boston."

"Come and see me, come and see me. I'll talk with you. Good day."

The lawyer went on his way. In one brief moment the world to Mark seemed spinning around. His breath came in quick struggling gasps, while wild possibilities surged through his brain, when he read the card in his hand which was that of a firm of lawyers whom he had often heard spoken of even in his far-off home.

The next morning Mark presented himself at the office and was kindly received by Mr. Brown. The lawyer glanced him over from head to foot. 'A good face', he thought, 'and pleasant way'. Then he noted the neat, cheap suit, the well-brushed hair and clean-looking skin. Then he asked a few direct, rapid questions, which Mark answered briefly.

"What can you do?"

"Plow, make a garden and read and write," dropping his voice over the two last accomplishments.

The lawyer laughed heartily.

"What's your name?"

"Mark Myers, suh."

"Well, Mark, I like your face, and your manner, too, my lad, and although its contrary to my way of doing — taking a boy without a reference — because of your honesty you may sit in as a porter and messenger here, if you've a mind to try the job. We want a boy just now, so you see you have struck it just right for yourself and me, too."

"If you are willing to take me, suh, just as you find me, I will do my best to please you," answered Mark, controlling his voice with an effort.

"Well, then, we'll consider it a bargain. I'll pay you what you are worth."

As Mark stepped across the threshold of the inner office and hung up his hat and coat he felt himself transformed. He was no longer a Negro! Henceforth he would be a white man in very truth. After all his plans, the metamorphosis had been accomplished by Fate. For the first time he seemed to live, to feel.

That night, he sat motionless beside the open window of the garret where he had found a lodging and planned his future.

"Oh, mammy," he cried at last, "if you knew you would forgive me. Some day you shall be rich." He broke off suddenly and dropped his head in his hands. Did he mean this, he asked himself in stern self-searching. His mother could not be mistaken for a white woman, her skin was light, but her hair and features were those of a Negress. He shuddered at the gulf he saw yawning between them. Nothing could bridge it. From now on she should no more exist as his mother for he had buried his old self that morning, and packed the earth hard above the coffin.

As the months went by a curious change came to the lad. This new life, this masquerade, so to speak, had become second nature. He looked at life from a white man's standpoint, and had assumed all of the prejudices and principles of the dominant race. Out of the careless boy had come a wary, taciturn man. He availed himself of the exceptional school privileges offered by night study in Boston, and improved rapidly. One morning, Mr. Brown came to Mark with good news. He had promoted him from porter to clerk, with a corresponding increase in his salary.

That night, Mark dreamed he was at home with his mother. He felt the loving touch of her toil-worn dusky hands, and heard the caressing tones of her voice in its soft Southern dialect. Ah, there had been such infinite peace in the old, careless, happy life he had led there. Pictures came and went before his mental vision with startling distinctness. He saw the modest log-cabin, the sweet-scented magnolia tree, the cotton fields, the sweeping long, gray moss hanging from the trees, the smell of the pines; he heard the cow-bells in the cane-brake, the hum of bees, and the sweet notes of the mocking-bird. He closed his eyes and could see the boys and girls dancing the old 'Virginia reel'. There's *Jinny Put the Kettle On*, and *Shoo! Miss Pijie, Shoo!* And then *King William Was King George's Son*, *Blind Man's Bluff*, and *Gimme Corner;* also *Walk the Lonesome Road:*

What the point was gittin kisses — shorz you born
The gals was dressed in homespun, long with their
brogan shoes,
And if their feet would touch you, you would feel,

*'Do' the boys wore bed-tuck breeches, these trifles was
forgot,
While joying up the ole Virginny reel.*

After that night he resolutely put by such thoughts; all
his associates were white, and his life was irrevocably
blended with the class far above the humble blacks.
Months rounded into years. At the end of five years,
Mark was on the road to wealth. He had studied law
and passed the Bar. A fortunate speculation in Western
land was the motive power that placed ten thousand
dollars in his pocket.

"So unexpected a windfall might have ruined some
men," Mr. Brown confided to his partner as they
smoked an after dinner cigar at Parker's, "but no fear
for Mark. His is an old head on young shoulders. He's
bound to be a power in the country before he dies."

"How about a 'Co.,' Brown? Ever thought of it in
connection with the firm? We aren't growing any
younger. What do you think of it?"

"Just the thing, Clark, Co. it is; and Myers is the
man."

The winter had set in early that year. Snow covered the
ground from the first of December. The air was biting
cold. The music of sleigh-bells, mingled with the voices
of children playing in the streets. There was good
skating on the frog pond and the Public Garden, where
the merry skaters glided to and fro in graceful circles

laughing and jesting merrily.

Down in the quarter where the colored people lived, Aunt Cloty sat most of the day looking drearily through the rusted iron railings of the area in a hopeless watch for a footstep that never came. Old, wrinkled, rheumatic, the patient face, and subdued air of the mulattress awakened sad feelings in the hearts of those who knew her story.

She had come North five years before searching for her son. At first she had been able to live in a humble way from her work as a laundress, but when sickness and old age laid their hands upon her, she had succumbed to the inevitable and subsisted upon the charity of the well-to-do among her neighbors, who had something to spare for a companion in poverty. After a time her case had come under the notice of the associated charities. At first it was determined to place the helpless creature in an institution where she could have constant attention, but her prayers and tears not to be carted to the poor-house, had stirred the pity of the officials and at length the attention of Lawyer Brown's daughter Katherine had been directed to Aunt Cloty as a worthy object of charity. Miss Brown was delighted with the quaintness of the old Negress and her tender heart overflowed with pity for her woes, and so the helpless woman became a welcome charge upon the purse of the petted favorite of fortune. Since that time better days had dawned for Aunt Cloty.

The wealthy girl and the old mulattress grew to be great friends. Every week found Katherine visiting her protégé sitting in the tiny room, listening eagerly to her tales of the sunny South.

Aunt Cloty's turban always seemed the insignia of her rank and proud pretensions, for she declared there was 'good blood' in her veins, and her majestic bearing testified to the truth of her words. When Cloty felt particularly humble, she laid the turban in flat folds on her head. In her character of a laundress, it was mounted a little higher. But when she received visitors, or called an enemy to account, the red flag of defiance towered aloft in wonderful proportion. So Miss Katherine could always read the signs of her protégé's feelings in the build of the red turban.

Christmas week the turban lay in flat folds and Cloty mourned aloud.

"He must be dead. 'Deed, chile, he must be dead or he'd never leave his ole mammy to suffer," she cried as she rocked her frail body in the old wooden rocker. Miss Katherine sat patiently listening.

"You see, Miss, Sonny's the only chile what I ever had. The good Lawd sent him to me like He done Isaac to take care of me, in my ole age, and since the night he ran off I ain't seed nothing but trouble. All that first year I was expecting him back again, and when the wind moaned round my cabin during the night, it seemed like I hear him calling for me, and I get up an open the door to listen, but it was dark and lonesome and he wasn't there. So, at last Marse Will, he says to me (Marse Will's one of my white folks, what I done nurse for two generations, and he call me mammy same as Sonny do),

'Mammy, Sonny's dead, or else he'd have written you where he was. Sonny has always been a good boy, and he wouldn't act no such way as this to you if he was living'. Yes, Miss, that's what Marse Will said, and it certainly did seem reasonable, but somehow I can't believe it." She paused, and opening an old carpet-sack always laid by her chair on the floor, drew from it a package. "This here is his little red coat and the first pair of britches he ever wore," she continued, displaying them to the young white girl with pride. "I fetched 'em North with me 'cause they keeps me company up here all alone."

Miss Katherine's swimming eyes attested her sympathy.

"He was the prettiest youngster," continued the old woman, with an upward tilt of her turbaned head, "and the day he put these on he strut, Miss, same as a peafowl."

"Aunt Cloty, I've told my father of your son and he's going to institute a search for him. If he's alive he'll find him for you, rest assured of that."

"God bless you, honey. God bless you. A big gentleman like the judge, your pa, will surely find him, for I believe Sonny's alive somewhere. Does I wanna see him?" and the woman's eyes held a joyous sparkle. "Does I want to see him? Why honey," coming close to the girl and unconsciously grasping her arm, "if he was in prison, and I couldn't get to him no other way, I'd be willing to crawl on my hands and knees as far again as I done come to get up North, just for one look at him."

For a moment she looked about her as though dazed, then some over-strained chord seemed to snap, and burying her face in her apron she sobbed aloud.

"No, Aunty, don't," and the impulsive heiress threw her soft arms about the forlorn figure and kissed the wrinkled face. "Tomorrow is Christmas Eve, and I am coming for you early in the day to take you home. You are to live with me after that, and if we don't find Sonny you shall never want while I live."

"I's heard of folks crying 'cause they're happy, but I ain't never done it. If I can just find Sonny I'll be the happiest old woman in the whole world."

And so it came about that Aunt Cloty was domiciled in the home of Judge Brown.

Christmas Eve in a great city is a wonderful sight The principal streets were in grand illumination. The shop windows were all ablaze, and through them came the vivid coloring of holiday gifts, tinting the coldness with an idea of warmth. It was a joyous pleasant scene; the pavements were thronged, and eager traffic was going on. A band of colored street musicians were passing from store to store stopping here and there to sing their peculiar songs to the accompaniment of guitars, banjos and bones. One trolled out in a powerful bass the notes of the old song:

The sun shines bright in my old Kentucky home,
'Tis summer the darkies are gay.

The familiar air fell upon the ears of a handsome dark-eyed man as he took his way leisurely through the throng. He paused a moment, dropped a coin in the hat extended for contributions, laughed, and hastened on his way. Presently he hummed the strain he had just heard in a rich undertone. Then there floated through his mind the fragments of a poem he had read somewhere:

> Hundreds of stars in the pretty sky;
> Hundreds of shells on the shore together;
> Hundreds of birds that go singing by;
> Hundreds of bees in sunny weather.
>
> Hundreds of dewdrops to greet the dawn;
> Hundreds of lambs in the purple clover;
> Hundreds of butterflies on the lawn;
> But only one mother the wide world over!

"Pshaw!" exclaimed Mark Myers as he pulled himself together and brushed aside unpleasant memories.

Katherine Brown had been walking restlessly up and down the great reception room. The sound of the bell reached her.

She stopped a moment, held her breath and listened. She heard Mark's voice in the hall and knew that her lover had come.

The servants were moving about in the back room, so she closed the folding-doors, and hid the Christmas tree, and sat down demurely waiting for him to come in, as if she had not indulged in a thought about the matter until then; though her heart was beating so tumultuously that a tuft of flowers among the lace on her bosom fluttered as if a breeze passed over it. The dainty room was redolent with the perfumes from a basket of tea-roses and Japan lilies that had been sent to the lovely girl as her first Christmas gift in the morning. Their fragrance pervaded the whole room, and it seemed that the fair owner moved through the calm of a tropical climate when she came forward to receive her guest; for that portion of her dress that swept the floor was rich with lace and summer-like in its texture, as if the blast of a storm could never reach her.

"My darling, you scarcely expected me, I am sure," said Myers coming forward with hand extended and a world of lovelight in his dark eyes, "but nothing would keep me from you tonight, foolish fellow that I am."

"I should never have forgiven you if you had not come," replied the girl with arched tenderness. "Why, sir, I have waited a half-hour already."

"Wondering what I should bring you for a Christmas gift?"

"No, not that," she answered, turning her eyes on the basket of flowers and blushing like a rose. "That came this morning, and I would let them put nothing else in the room, for your roses turned it into a little heaven of my own."

"They will perish in a day or two at best. But I have really brought you something that will keep its own as long as we two shall love each other."

"So long! Then it will be perfect to all eternity."

Mark grew serious. Something in her words struck him with a thought of death; a chill passed over him.

"God forbid that it should not remain so while you and I live Katherine; for see, it is the engagement ring I have brought you."

A flood of crimson rose to her face. The little hand held out for the ring, quivering like a leaf. She held the star-like solitaire in her hand a moment, gazing on it with reverence, scarcely conscious of its beauty. It might have been a lot of glass rather than a limpid diamond for anything she thought of the matter, she only knew how solemn and sacred a thing that jewel was.

"No, you must put it on first," she said, resting one hand softly on his breast, and holding the ring toward him. "I shall always love it better if taken from your own fingers."

Myers gazing down into her face, read all the solemn and beautiful thoughts that prompted the action, and his own sympathetic nature was subdued by them into solemn harmony.

As he stood before her submitting one hand to her sweet will, he whispered, "And you are happy, my beloved?"

"Happy! Oh, Mark, if we could always be so, heaven would begin here with you. Nothing can part us now, we are irrevocably bound to each other forever. If only the whole world could be happy as we are tonight."

Her words jarred upon him an instant. His old

mother's face rose before him as it had not done for years.

"Come," said Katherine, "let me show you the Christmas tree; papa and Aunt Cloty are just finishing it."

As she spoke she threw wide the doors and in the midst of a the glitter and dazzle he heard a voice scream out:

"Oh, my God! It's him! It's my boy! It's Sonny!"

Then panting excitedly, arms extended, the yellow face suffused with tenderness, Mark saw his mother standing before him.

After that scream came a deathly silence, Mark stood as if carved into stone, in an instant he saw his life in ruins, Katherine lost to him, chaos about the social fabric of his life. He could not do it. Then with a long breath he set his teeth bud opened his lips to denounce her as crazy, but in that instant his eyes fell on her drawn face, and quivering lips. In another moment he saw his conduct of the past years in all its hideousness. Suddenly Judge Brown spoke.

"Mark, what is this? Have you nothing to say?"

He would not glance at Katherine. One look at her fair face would unman him. He turned slowly and faced Judge Brown and there was defiance in his look. All that was noble in his nature spoke at last.

Another instant his arms were about his fond old mother, while she sobbed her heart out on his breast.

AFTER MANY DAYS
Fannie Bamer Williams

Christmas on the Edwards plantation, as it was still
called, was a great event to old and young, master and
slave comprising the Edwards household. Although
freedom had long ago been declared, many of the older
slaves could not be induced to leave the plantation,
chiefly because the Edwards family had been able to
maintain their appearance of opulence through the
vicissitudes of war, and the subsequent disasters, which
had impoverished so many of their neighbors. It is one
of the peculiar characteristics of the American Negro
that he is never to be found in large numbers in any
community where the white people are as poor as
himself. It is, therefore, not surprising that the Edwards
plantation had no difficulty in retaining nearly all of
their former slaves as servants under the new regime.

The stately Edwards mansion, with its massive
pillars, and spreading porticoes, gleaming white in its

setting of noble pines and cedars, is still the pride of a certain section of old Virginia.

One balmy afternoon a few days before the great Christmas festival, Doris Edwards, the youngest granddaughter of this historic southern home, was hastening along a well-trodden path leading down to an old white-washed cabin, one of the picturesque survivals of plantation life before the war. The pathway was bordered on either side with old-fashioned flowers, some of them still lifting a belated blossom, caught in the lingering balm of Autumn, while faded stalks of hollyhock and sunflower, like silent sentinels, guarded the door of this humble cabin.

Through the open vine-latticed window, Doris sniffed with keen delight the mingled odor of pies, cakes and various other dainties temptingly spread out on the snowy kitchen table waiting to be conveyed to the main house to contribute to the coming Christmas cheer.

Peering into the gloomy cabin, Doris discovered old Aunt Linda, with whom she had always been a great favorite, sitting in a low chair before the old brick oven, her apron thrown over her head, swaying back and forth to the doleful measure of a familiar plantation melody, to which the words, "Lambs of the Upper Fold," were being paraphrased in a most ludicrous way. As far back as Doris could remember, it had been an unwritten law on the plantation that when Aunt Linda's 'blues chile' reached the 'Lambs Of The Upper Fold' stage, she was in a mood not to be trifled with.

Aunt Linda had lived on the plantation so long she had become quite a privileged character. It had never been known just how she had learned to read and write, but this fact had made her a kind of a leader among the other servants, and had earned for herself greater respect even from the Edwards family. Having been a house servant for many years, her language was also better than the other servants, and her spirits were very low indeed, when she lapsed into the language of the 'quarters'. There was also a tradition in the family that Aunt Linda's coming to the plantation had from the first been shrouded in mystery. In appearance she was a tall yellow woman, straight as an Indian, with piercing black eyes, and bearing herself with a certain dignity of manner, unusual in a slave. Visitors to the Edwards place would at once single her out from among the other servants, sometimes asking some very uncomfortable questions concerning her Doris, however, was the one member of the household who refused to take Aunt Linda's moods seriously, so taking in the situation at a glance, she determined to put an end to this mood at least. Stealing softly upon the old woman, she drew the apron from her head, exclaiming, "Oh, Aunt Linda. Just leave your 'lambs' alone for today, won't you? This is Christmas time, and I have left all kinds of nice things going on up at the house to bring you the latest news. What is the matter anyway?"

The old woman slowly raised her head, saying, "I might have known it was you, you certainly is getting mighty saucy, chile, how you did fright me sure. My mind was way back in ole Carolina, just before another Christmas, when the Lord done lay one hand on my poor heart, and with the other press down the white lids over the blue eyes of my sweet Alice. Oh, my chile, can I ever forget that day?"

Doris, fearing another outburst, interrupted the moans of the old woman by playfully placing her hand over her mouth, saying: "Wait a minute, auntie, I want to tell you something. There are so many delightful people up to the house, but I want to tell you about two of them especially. Sister May has just come and has brought with her her friend, Pauline Sommers, who sings beautifully, and she is going to sing our Christmas carol for us on Christmas Eve. With them is the loveliest girl I ever saw, her name is Gladys Winne. I wish I could describe her, but I can't. I can only remember her violet eyes; think of it, auntie, not blue, but violet, just like the pansies in your garden last summer."

At the mention of the last name, Aunt Linda rose, leaning on the table for support. It seemed to her as if some cruel hand had reached out of a pitiless past and clutched her heart. Doris gazed in startled awe at the storm of anguish that seemed to sweep across the old woman's face, exclaiming "Why, auntie, are you sick?"

In a hoarse voice, she answered, "Yes, chile, yes, I am sick."

This poor old slave woman's life was rimmed by just two events, a birth and a death, and even these memories were hers and not hers, yet the mention of a single name has for a moment blotted out all the intervening years and in another lowly cabin, the name of Gladys is whispered by dying lips to breaking hearts. Aunt Linda gave a swift glance at the startled Doris, while making a desperate effort to recall her wandering thoughts, lest unwittingly she betray her loved ones to this little chatterer. Forcing a ghastly smile, she said, as if to herself, "As if there was only one Gladys in all this world, yes and heaps of Winnes, too, I reckon. Go on chile, go on. Ole Aunt Linda is sure getting ole and silly."

Doris left the cabin bristling with curiosity, but fortunately for Aunt Linda, she would not allow it to worry her pretty head very long.

The lovely Gladys Winne, as she was generally called, was indeed the most winsome and charming of all the guests that composed the Christmas party in the Edwards mansion. Slightly above medium height, with a beautifully rounded form, delicately poised head crowned with rippling chestnut hair, curling in soft tendrils about neck and brow, a complexion of dazzling fairness with the tint of the rose in her cheeks, and the whole face lighted by deeply glowing violet eyes. Thus liberally endowed by nature, there was further added the charm of a fine education, the advantage of foreign travel, contact with brilliant minds, and a social prestige through her foster parents, that fitted her for the most exclusive social life.

She had recently been betrothed to Paul Westlake, a handsome, wealthy and gifted young lawyer of New York. He had been among the latest arrivals, and

Gladys' happiness glowed in her expressive eyes, and fairly scintillated from every curve of her exquisite form. Beautifully gowned in delicate blue of soft and clinging texture draped with creamy lace, she was indeed as rare a picture of radiant youth and beauty as one could wish to see.

Gladys' happiness was not without problem. She had one real or fancied annoyance, which she could not shake off, though she tried not to think about it. But as she walked with Paul, through the rambling rooms of this historic mansion, she determined to call his attention to it.

They had just passed an angle near a stairway, when Gladys nervously pressed his arm, saying, "Look, Paul, do you see that tall yellow woman; she follows me everywhere, and actually haunts me like a shadow. If I turn suddenly, I can just see her gliding out of sight. Sometimes she becomes bolder, and coming closer to me, she peers into my face as if she would look me through. Really there seems to be something uncanny about it all to me; it makes me shiver. Look, Paul, there she is now, even your presence does not daunt her."

Paul, after satisfying himself that she was really serious and annoyed, ceased laughing, saying, "My darling, I cannot consistently blame anyone for looking at you. It may be due to an inborn curiosity; she probably is attracted by other lovely things in the same way, only you may not have noticed it."

"Nonsense," said Gladys, blushing, "that is a very sweet explanation, but it doesn't explain in this case. It annoys me so much that I think I must speak to Mrs Edwards about it."

Here Paul quickly interrupted.

"No, my dear, I would not do that; she is evidently a privileged servant, judging from the right of way she seems to have all over the house. Mrs. Edwards is very kind and gracious to us, yet she might resent any criticism of her servants. Try to dismiss it from your mind, my love. I have always heard that these old mammies are very superstitious, and she may fancy that she has seen you in some vision or dream, but it ought not to cause you any concern at all. Just fix your mind on something pleasant; on me, for instance."

Thus lovingly rebuked and comforted, Gladys did succeed in forgetting for a time her silent watcher. But the thing that annoyed her almost more than anything else was the fact that she had a sense of being irresistibly drawn towards this old servant, by a chord of sympathy and interest, for which she could not in any way account.

But the fatal curiosity of her sex, despite the advice of Paul, whom she so loved and trusted, finally wrought her own undoing. The next afternoon, at a time when she was sure she would not be missed, Gladys stole down to Aunt Linda's cabin determined to probe this mystery for herself. Finding the cabin door ajar, she slipped lightly into the room.

Aunt Linda was so absorbed by what she was doing that she heard no sound. Gladys paused upon the threshold of the cabin, fascinated by the old woman's strange occupation. She was bending over the contents of an old hair chest, tenderly shaking out one little garment after another of a baby's wardrobe, filling the room with the pungent odor of camphor and lavender.

The tears were falling and she would hold the little garments to her bosom, crooning some quaint cradle song, tenderly murmuring, "Oh, my lamb, my poor little lamb," and then, as if speaking to someone unseen, she would say, "No, my darling, no, your ole mother will surely never break her promise to young master. If you could only see how lovely your little Gladys has grown to be! Sweet innocent Gladys and her poor ole granma must not speak to or touch her, must not tell her how her own ma loved her and that these ole hands was the first to hold her, and mine the first kiss she ever knew. Oh my darling, I will never betray you, she shall never know."

Then the old woman's sobs would break out afresh, as she frantically clasped the tiny garments, yellow with age, but dainty enough for a princess, to her aching heart.

For a moment Gladys, fresh and sweet as a flower, felt only the tender sympathy of a casual observer, for what possible connection could there be between her and this old colored woman in her sordid surroundings. Unconsciously she drew her skirts about her in scorn of the bare suggestion, but the next moment found her transfixed with horror, a sense of approaching doom enveloping her as in a mist. Clutching at her throat, and with dilated unseeing eyes, she groped her way toward the old woman, violently shaking her, while in a terror-stricken voice she cried, "Oh Aunt Linda, what is it?"

With a cry like the last despairing groan of a wounded animal, Aunt Linda dropped upon her knees, scattering a shower of filmy lace and dainty flannels about her. Through every fibre of her being, Gladys felt the absurdity of her fears, yet in spite of herself, the words welled up from her heart to her lips, "Oh Aunt Linda, what is it, what have I to do with your dead?" With an hysterical laugh, she added, "Do I look like someone you have loved and lost in other days?"

Then the simple-hearted old woman, deceived by the kindly note in Gladys' voice, and not seeing the unspeakable horror growing in her eyes, stretched out imploring hands as to a little child, the tears streaming from her eyes, saying, "Oh, Gladys." not Miss Gladys now, as the stricken girl quickly notes, "you is my own sweet Alice's little chile, Oh, honey I am your own dear granma. You're beautiful, Gladys, but not more so than your own sweet ma, who loved you so."

The old woman was so happy to be relieved of the secret burden she had borne for so many years, that she had almost forgotten Gladys' presence, until she saw her lost darling fainting before her very eyes. Quickly she caught her in her arms, tenderly pillowing her head upon her ample bosom, where as a little babe she had so often lain.

For several minutes the gloomy cabin was wrapped in solemn silence. Finally Gladys raised her head, and turning toward Aunt Linda her face, from which every trace of youth and happiness had fled, in a hoarse and almost breathless whisper, said: "If you are my own grandmother, who then was my father?" Before this searching question these two contrasted types of southern conditions, stood dumb and helpless. The shadow of the departed crime of slavery still remained to haunt the generations of freedom.

Though Aunt Linda had known for many years that she was free, the generous kindness of the Edwards family had made the Emancipation proclamation almost meaningless to her.

When she now realised that the fatal admission, which had brought such gladness to her heart, had only deepened the horror in Gladys' heart, a new light broke upon her darkened mind. Carefully placing Gladys in a chair, the old woman raised herself to her full height, her right hand uplifted like a bronze goddess of liberty. For the first time and for a brief moment she felt the inspiring thrill and meaning of the term freedom. Ignorant of almost everything as comes with the knowledge and experience of the stricken girl before her, yet a revelation of the sacred relationships of parenthood, childhood and home, the common heritage of all humanity swept aside all differences of complexion or position.

For one moment, despite her lowly surroundings, an equality of blood, nay superiority of blood, tingled in old Aunt Linda's veins, straightened her body, and flashed her eye. But the crushing process of over two centuries could not sustain in her more than a moment

of asserted womanhood. Slowly she lowered her arm
and, with bending body, she was again but an old slave
woman with haunting memories and a bleeding heart.
Then with tears and broken words, she poured out the
whole pitiful story to the sobbing Gladys.

"It was this way, honey, it all happened just before
the war, way down in ole Carolina. My little Alice, my
one chile had grown up to be so beautiful. Even when
she was a tiny little chile, I used to look at her and
wonder how the good Lord ever 'lowed her to slip over
my door sill, but never mind that chile, that is not you
alls concern. When she was 'bout seventeen years ole,
she was so pretty that the white folks was always asking
of me if she was my own chile, the idea, as if her own
ma, but then that was all right for them, it was just
because she was so white, I knowd.

"Tho' I lived with my little Alice in the cabin, I was
the housemaid in the big house, but I'd never let Alice
be up there with me when there was company, in case,
well, I just had to be careful, never mind why. But one
day, young Master Harry Winne was home from school,
and they were celebrating, and I was in a hurry; so I set
Alice to bringing some roses from the garden to trim the
table, and there young master saw her, and came after
me to know who she was; he say he thought he knowed
all his ma's company, then I guess I was too proud, and
I up and tells him that she was my Alice, my own little
gal, and I was right away scared that I had told him, but
he had seen her; that was enough, Oh my poor lamb!"
Here the old woman paused, giving herself up for a

moment to unrestrained weeping. Suddenly she dried her eyes and said, "Gladys, chile, does you know what love is?"

Gladys' cheeks made eloquent response, and with one swift glance, the old woman continued.

"Then you knows how they loved each other. One day Master Harry went to ole Master and he say, 'Father, I know you'll be awful angered at me, but I will marry Alice or no woman'. Then his father say — but never mind what he said, only it was enough to make young master say that he'd never forgive his pa for what he said about my little gal.

"Some time after that my Alice began to droop and pine away, so one day I said to her, 'Alice, does you and young master love each other'? Then she told me that young master had married her, and that she was afraid to tell even her ma, case they might send him away from her forever. When young master came again he told me all about it; just like my girl had told me. He said he could not live without her. After that be would steal down to see her when he could, bringing her all these pretty laces and things, and she would sit all day and cry like her heart would break.

"He would bribe ole Sam not to tell ole Master, saying that he was soon going to take her away where no men could touch them. Well, after you was born, she began to fade away from me, getting weaker every day. Then when you was only a few months ole (oh, how she worshipped you) I saw that my poor unhappy little girl was going on that long journey away from her poor heart-broke ma, to that home not made with hands, then I sent for young master, your pa. Oh, how he begged her not to go, saying that he had a home all ready for her an you up North. Gently she laid you in his arms, sure the most beautiful chile that ever were, with your big violet eyes looking up into his, tho' he could not see them for the tears that would fall on your sweet face. Your ma tried to smile, reaching out her weak arms for you, she said: 'Gladys,' and with choking sobs she made us both promise that you shall never know that your family were slaves or that she has a drop of my blood: 'Make it all yours, Harry, never let her know', she said. We both promised, and that night young master tore you from my breaking heart 'cause it was best. After I had laid away my poor unhappy chile, I begged ole Master to sell me, so as to send me way off to Virginia, where I could never trace you nor look for you, and I never have."

Then the old woman threw herself upon her knees, wringing her hands and saying, "Oh my God, why did you let her find me?"

She had quite forgotten Gladys' presence in the extremity of her distress at having broken her vow to the dead and perhaps wrought sorrow for the living.

Throughout the entire recital, told between heart-breaking sobs and moans, Gladys sat as if carved in marble, never removing her eyes from the old woman's face. Slowly she aroused herself, allowing her dull eyes to wander about the room at the patchwork covered bed in the corner; then through the open casement, from which she could catch a glimpse of a group of young Negroes, noting their coarse features and boisterous play; then back again to the crouching, sobbing old woman. With a shiver running through her entire form, she found her voice, which seemed to come from a great distance, "And I am part of all this! Oh, my God, how can I live; above all, how can I tell Paul, but I must and will. I will not deceive him though it kills me."

At the sound of Gladys' voice Aunt Linda's faculties awoke, and she began to realise the awful possibilities of her divulged secrets. Aunt Linda had felt and known the horrors of slavery but could she have known that after twenty years of freedom nothing in the whole range of social disgraces could work such terrible disinheritance to man or woman as the presence of Negro blood, seen or unseen, she would have given almost life itself rather than to have condemned this darling of her love and prayers to so dire a fate.

The name of Paul, breathed by Gladys in accents of such tenderness and despair, aroused Aunt Linda to action. She implored her not to tell Paul or anyone else.

"No one need ever know, no one ever can or shall know," she pleaded. "How could any find out, honey, if you did not tell them?" Then seizing one of Gladys' little hands, pink and white and delicate as a rose leaf, and placing it beside her own old and yellow one, she cried, "Look chile, look, could anyone ever find the same blood in these two hands by just looking at 'em? No, honey, I have kept this secret all these years, and now pass it on to you and you must keep it for yourself

'til the end of time, 'deed you must, no one need ever
know."

To her dying day Aunt Linda never forgot the
despairing cry of this stricken girl, as she said, "What
have I done to deserve this?"

With no word of pity for the suffering old woman,
she clutched her arm, saying in a stifled whisper,
"Again, who was, or is my father, and where is he?"

Aunt Linda cowered before this angry goddess,
though she was of her own flesh and blood, and softly
said: "He is dead; died when you were about five years
old. He left you heaps of money, and in the care of a
childless couple, who reared you like their own. He
made 'em let you keep his name, I can't see why."

With the utmost contempt Gladys cried, "Gold, gold,
what is gold to such a heritage as this? An ocean of gold
cannot wash away this stain."

Poor Gladys never knew how she reached her room.
She turned to lock the door, resolved to fight this battle
out for herself; then she thought of kind Mrs. Edwards.
She would never need a mother's love so much as now.
Of her own mother, she dared not even think. Then, too,
why had she thought of it before, this horrible story
might not be true. Aunt Linda was probably out of her
mind. Mrs. Edwards would surely know.

By a striking coincidence Mrs. Edwards had noticed
Linda's manner toward her fair guest, and knowing the
old woman's connection with the Winne family, she had
just resolved to send for her and question her as to her
suspicions, if she had any, and at least caution her as to

her manner.

Hearing a light tap upon her door, she hastily opened it. She needed but one glance at Gladys' unhappy countenance to tell her that it was too late; the mischief had already been done. With a cry of pity and dismay, Mrs. Edwards opened her arms and Gladys swooned upon her breast. Tenderly she laid her down and when she had regained consciousness, she sprang up, crying, "Oh Mrs. Edwards, say that it is not true, that it is some horrible dream from which I shall soon awaken?"

How gladly would this good woman have sacrificed almost anything to spare this lovely girl, the innocent victim of an outrageous and blighting system, but Gladys was now a woman and must be answered.

"Gladys, my dear," said Mrs. Edwards, "I wish I might save you further distress, by telling you that what I fear you have heard, perhaps from Aunt Linda herself, is not true. I am afraid it is all too true. But fortunately in your case no one need know. It will be safe with us and I will see that Aunt Linda does not mention it again, she ought not to have admitted it to you."

Very gently Mrs. Edwards confirmed Aunt Linda's story, bitterly inveighing against a system which mocked at marriage vows, even allowing a man to sell his own flesh and blood for gain. She told this chaste and delicate girl how poor slave girls, many of them most beautiful in form and feature, were not allowed to be modest, not allowed to follow the instinct of moral rectitude, that they might be held at the mercy of their

masters. Poor Gladys writhed as if under the lash. She
little knew what painful reasons Mrs. Edwards had for
hating the entire system of debasement to both master
and slave.

Her kind heart, southern born and bred as she was,
yearned to give protection and home to two beautiful
girls, who had shut out from her own hearthstone,
which by right of birth and honor was theirs to share
also.

"Tell me, Gladys, which race is the more to be
despised? Forgive dear, for telling you these things, but
my mind was haunted by very bitter memories. Though
great injustice was done, and is still being done, I say to
you, my child, from selfish interest and the peace of my
household, I will not allow such a disgrace to attach to
one of my most respected guests. Do you not then see,
dear, the unwisdom of revealing your identity here and
now? Unrevealed, we are all friends."

The covert threat lurking in the unfinished voice was
not lost upon Gladys. She arose, making an attempt to
be calm, but nervously seizing Mrs. Edwards' hand.

"Have I no living white relatives?" she asked.

Mrs. Edwards waited a moment, then said, "Yes, a
few, but they are very shy and influential, and now
living in the north; so that I very much afraid that they
are not concerned as to hear you are living or not. They
knew, of course, of your birth; but since the death of
your father, whom they all loved much, I have heard,
though it may be only gossip, that they do not now
allow your name to be mentioned."

Gladys searched Mrs. Edwards' face with a peculiarly perplexed look; then in a plainer tone of voice, said, "Mrs. Edwards, it must be that only Negroes possess natural affection. Think of it, through all the years of my life, and though I have many near relatives, I have been cherished and yearned for by only one of them, and she is a despised colored woman. The almost infinitesimal drop of her blood in my veins is really the only drop that I can consistently be proud of." Then, springing up, an indescribable glow fairly transfiguring and illuminating her face, she said, "My kind hostess, and comforting friend, I feel that I must tell Paul, but for your sake we will say nothing to the others, and if he does not advise me, yes, command me, to own and cherish that lonely old woman's love, and make happy her declining years, then he is not the man to whom I can or will entrust my love and life."

With burning cheeks, and eyes hiding the stars in their violet depths, her whole countenance glowing with a sense of pride conquered and love exalted, beautiful to see, she turned to Mrs. Edwards and tenderly kissing her, passed softly from the room.

For several moments, Mrs. Edwards stood where Gladys had left her.

"Poor deluded girl," she mused. "Paul Westlake is by far one of the truest and noblest young men I have ever known, but let him beware, for there is even now coming to meet him the strongest test of his manhood principles he has ever had to face; beside it, all other perplexing problems must sink into nothingness. Will he be equal to it? We shall soon see."

Gladys, in spite of the sublime courage that had so exalted her but a moment before, felt her resolution weaken with every step. It required almost a super-human will to resist the temptation to silence, so eloquently urged upon her by Mrs. Edwards. But her resolution was not to be thus lightly set aside; it pursued her to her room, translating itself into the persistent thought that if fate is ever to be met and conquered, the time is now; delays are dangerous.

As she was about to leave her room on her mission, compelled by an indefinable sense of farewell, she turned, with her hand upon the door, as if she would include in this backward glance all the dainty furnishings, the taste and elegance everywhere displayed, and of which she had felt very much a part. Finally her wandering gaze fell upon a fine picture of Paul Westlake upon the mantel. Instantly there into her mind came the first and only public address she had ever heard Paul make. She had quite forgotten the occasion, except that it had some relation to a so-called 'Negro problem'. Then out from the past came the rich tones of the beloved voice as with fervid eloquence he arraigned the American people for the wrongs and injustice that had been perpetrated upon a weak and defenseless people through centuries of their enslavement and their few years of freedom.

With much feeling he recounted the pathetic story of this unhappy people when freedom found them, trying to knit together the broken ties of family kinship and their struggles through all the odds and hates of opposition, trying to make a place for themselves in the great family of races. Gladys' awakened conscience quickens the memory of his terrible condemnation of a system and of the men who would willingly demoralize a whole race of women, even at the sacrifice of their own flesh and blood.

With Mrs. Edwards' words still ringing in her ears, the memory of the last few words stings her now as then, except that now she knows why she is so sensitive as to their real import.

This message brought to her from out a happy past by Paul's pictured face, has given to her a light of hope and comfort beyond words. Hastily closing the door of her room, almost eagerly, and with buoyant step, she went to seek Paul and carry out her mission.

To Paul Westlake's loving heart, Gladys Winne never appeared so full of beauty, curves and graces, her eyes glowing with confidence and love, as when he sprang eagerly forward to greet her on that eventful afternoon. Through all the subsequent years of their lives the tenderness and beauty of that afternoon together never faded from their minds.

They seemed, though surrounded by the laughter of friends and festive preparations, quite alone, set apart by the intensity of their love and happiness.

When they were about to separate for the night, Gladys turned to Paul, with ominous seriousness, yet trying to assume a lightness she was far from feeling, saying, "Paul, dear, I am going to put your love to the test tomorrow, may I?" Paul's smiling indifference was surely test enough, if that were all, but she persisted, "I am quite in earnest, dear, I have a confession to make to you. I intended to tell you this afternoon, but I could not cloud our last evening together for a long time perhaps, so I decided to ask you to meet me in the library tomorrow morning at ten o'clock will you?" '

"Will I," Paul replied, "my darling, you know I will do anything you ask.But why tomorrow, and why so serious about the matter? Besides, if it be anything that is to affect our future in any way, why not tell it now?"

As Gladys was still silent, he added, "Dear, if you will assure me that this confession will not change your love for me in any way, I will willingly wait until tomorrow or next year, any time can you give me this assurance?"

Gladys softly answered, "Yes, Paul, my love is yours now and always; that is, if you will always wish it."

There was an expression upon her face he did not like, because he could not understand it, but tenderly drawing her to him, he said, "Gladys, dear, can anything matter so long as we love each other? I truly believe it cannot. But tell me this, dear, after this confession do I then hold the key to the situation?"

"Yes, Paul, I believe you do; in fact I know that you will."

"Ah, that is one point gained, tomorrow; then it can have no terrors for me," he lightly replied.

Gladys passed an almost sleepless night. Confident, yet fearful, she watched the dawn of the new day. Paul, on the contrary, slept peacefully and rose to greet the morn with confidence and cheer.

"If I have Gladys' love," he mused, "there is nothing in heaven or earth for me to fear."

At last the dreaded hour of ten drew near; their 'Ides of March' Paul quoted with some amusement over the situation. The first greeting over, the silence became oppressive. Paul broke it at last, saying briskly, "Now, dear, out with this confession. I am not a success at conundrums; another hour of this suspense would have been my undoing," he laughingly said.

Gladys, pale and trembling, felt all of her courage slipping from her; she knew not how to begin. Although she had rehearsed every detail of this scene again and again, she could not recall a single word she had intended to say. Finally she began with the reminder she had intended to use as a last resort, "Paul, do you remember taking me last Spring to hear your first public address? Do you remember how eloquently and earnestly you pleaded the cause of the Negro?" Seeing only a growing perplexity upon his face, she cried, "My love, can you not see what I am trying to say? Oh, do you not understand? But no, no one could ever guess a thing so awful." Then sinking her voice almost to a whisper and with averted face, she said, "Paul, it was because you were unconsciously pleading for your own Gladys, for I am one of them."

"What nonsense is this," exclaimed Paul, springing from his chair, "it is impossible, worse than improbable, it cannot be true. It is the work of some jealous rival.

Surely, Gladys, you do not expect me to believe such a wild, unthinkable story as this!" Then controlling himself, he said, "Oh, my darling, who could have been so cruel as to have tortured you like this? If any member of this household has done this thing let us leave them in this hour. I confess I do not love the South or a Southerner, with my whole heart, in spite of this 'united country' nonsense; yes, I will say it, and in spite of the apparently gracious hospitality of this household."

Gladys, awed by the violence of his indignation, placed a trembling hand upon his arm, saying, "Listen, Paul, do you not remember on the very evening of your arrival here, of my calling your attention to a tall turbaned servant with piercing eyes? Don't you remember I told you how she annoyed me by following me everywhere, and you laughed away my fears, and lovingly quieted my alarm? Now, Paul, how can I say it, but I must; that woman, that Negress, who was once a slave, is my own grandmother." Without waiting for him to reply, she humbly but bravely poured into his ears the whole pitiful story, sparing neither father nor mother, but blaming her mother least of all. Ah the pity of it!

Without a word, Paul took hold of her trembling hands and drawing her toward the window, with shaking hand, he drew aside the heavy drapery; then turning her face so that the full glory of that sunlit morning fell upon it, he looked long and searchingly into the beautiful beloved face, as if studying the minutest detail of some matchless piece of statuary. At last he found words, saying: "You, my flower, is it possible that there can be concealed in this flawless skin, these dear violet eyes, these finely chiseled features, a trace of lineage or blood, without a single characteristic to vindicate its presence? I will not believe it; it cannot be true." Then baffled by Gladys' silence, he added, "And if it be true, surely the Father of us all intended to leave no hint of shame or dishonor on this, the fairest of his creations."

Gladys felt rather than heard a deepened note of tenderness in his voice and her hopes revived. Then suddenly his calm face whitened and an expression terrible to see swept over it.

Instinctively Gladys read his thought. She knew that the last unspoken thought was of the future, and because she, too, realised that the problem of heredity must be settled outside the realm of sentiment, her breaking heart made quick.

For some moments they sat in unbroken silence; then Gladys spoke: "Goodbye, Paul, I see that you must wrestle with this life problem alone as I have; there is no other way. But that you may be wholly untrammelled in your judgment, I want to assure you that you are free. I love you too well to willingly degrade your name and prospects by contaminating them with a taint of blood, of which I was as innocent as yourself, until two days ago.

"May I ask you to meet me once more, and for the last time, at twelve o'clock tonight? I will then abide by your judgment as to what is best for both of us. Let us

try to be ourselves today, so that our own heartaches
may not cloud the happiness of others. I said twelve
o'clock because I thought it would be less apt to be
missed at that hour than at any other time. Goodbye,
dear, 'til then."

Absently Paul replied "All right, Gladys, just as you
say; I'll be here."

At the approach of the midnight hour, Paul and
Gladys made their way to the library, which had
become to them a solemn and sacred trysting place.

Gladys looked luminously beautiful on this
Christmas Eve. She wore a black gauze dress flecked
with silver, through which her skin gleamed with
dazzling fairness. Her only ornaments were sprigs of
holly, their brilliant berries adding the necessary touch
of color to her unusual pallor. She greeted him with
gentle sweetness and added dignity and courage in her
eyes.

Eagerly she scanned his countenance and sought his
eyes and then she shrank back in dismay at his set face
and stern demeanor.

Suddenly the strength of her love for him and the
glory and tragedy which his love had brought to her life
surged through her, breaking down all reserve.

"Look at me, Paul," she cried in a tense whisper,
"have I changed since yesterday? Am I not the same
Gladys you have loved so long?"

In a moment their positions had changed and she
had become the forceful advocate at the bar of love and
justice; the love of her heart overwhelmed her voice

with a torrent of words she implored him by the sweet and sacred memories that had enkindled from the first their mutual love, by the remembered kisses, their afterglow flooding her cheeks as she spoke, and "Oh, my love, the happy days together," she paused, as if the very sweetness of the memory oppressed her voice to silence, and helpless and imploring she held out her hands to him.

Paul was gazing at her as if entranced, a growing tenderness filling and thrilling his soul. Gradually he became conscious of a tightening of the heart at the thought of losing her out of his life. There could be no such thing as life without Gladys, and when would she need his love, his protection, his tenderest sympathy so much as now?

The light upon Paul's transfigured countenance is reflected on Gladys' own and as he moves toward her with outstretched arms. In the adjoining room the magnificent voice of the beautiful singer rises in the Christmas carol, mingling in singular harmony with the plaintive melody as sung by a a group of dusky singers beneath the windows.

THE FOLLY OF MILDRED
Ruth D. Todd

"Mildred James is the most ill-bred girl in the neighborhood, and I think it would be very foolish as well as quite useless to include her name."

The speaker was Lillian Jones, a tall, pretty girl with light brown complexion. Her companion was Laura Claire, who, if not quite so pretty, was nevertheless graceful and tall, and her plain dark face was lighted by a pair of soft, lustrous, almost fascinating dark eyes.

"That is just where we differ, Lillie. We must not exclude Miss James. On the contrary, her name should head the list," answered Laura, as she regarded her with a steady, reproving

Both young girls were seated before a writing table which was strewn with paper, pens and ink. Laura was writing, and Lillian was glancing over and inspecting each little note which was intended for the different girls of their exclusive circle.

"My dear Laura," exclaimed Lillian, rather impatiently, "you can't be serious. Why, the mere name of this would spoil the reputation of the entire club. You forget all the slighting remarks that are made regarding her character?"

Laura laid down her pen and gazed steadily out of the window for quite a few moments before replying. Then thing her gentle eyes full upon Lillian, she said, "No, I have not forgotten the rumors afloat, and that is the very reason why she should belong to this club."

Lillian gazed at her incredulously.

"Dear me, you are extremely exasperating sometimes! It would better become us to erase the name 'social' from our club and place 'reform' in its stead, it would certainly be more appropriate, from your point of view at all events. Besides, we could go around town and hunt up all the disreputable girls and reform them."

"Please spare me your sarcasm, Lillie, and listen to reason."

But Lillian interrupted her impatiently.

"I hate reasoning about Mildred James. You know yourself, Laura, that she is so conceited and overbearing that at times she scarcely notices either of us. I hate this 'color line' nonsense within our own race. It's bad enough to have a dividing line between the Negro and the Caucasian, but when it comes to one Negro ignoring another simply because their Anglo-Saxon blood is not so prominent, I lose all patience as well as respect for them unless they are ignorant. And you know, Laura, that there is no excuse for Mildred James. She has an excellent education, and despite the whispered comments and slighting remarks upon her reputation, she moves in good circles," exclaimed Lillian with ardor.

Laura gazed at her with a significant smile, and when she had finished she quietly replied, "You are right, I dare say. At all events, what you have just said has a ring of solid fact. But that doesn't show that we must exclude her name.

"She is well-educated, as you before stated, but she must join this club, as only through this medium can she be reduced to a sense of her shame. She must know that even though she is a graduate of the normal school, she is still extremely ignorant in many ways. She must be made to understand that her tastes and manners are forced and exaggerated, her mind decidedly uncultivated, and her morals in sad need of repair. It is not to be wondered at that the colored American girl is regarded by the Anglo-Saxon as utterly devoid of all morality when such girls as Miss James (as well as many others I could name), display such shameful conduct and set such disgraceful examples. Must we, then, stand calmly by and receive upon our shoulders the burden of more unfortunate sisters' disgrace without one protest? Decidedly not. It Is our duty to show the world that there are a countless number of virtuous dark-skinned women. And this we can only accomplish by co-operation. Together we must try to advise and reform our straying sisters, at the same time leading the younger ones in the path of virtue and womanly modesty. Consequently, we must reach out our hands and grasp that of those who have not completely gone astray, through the medium of this club. For although it bears the title of 'Social', morals, social reform, literature, elocution and latter-day etiquette are to be studied deeply, and discussed thoroughly."

"I had not looked at it in that light, Laura. I don't suppose any of the other girls would have studied the subject so deeply either. Your arguments are extremely convincing. But there are many reform clubs for straying girls, besides, I don't think that any of the other girls will be so deeply impressed as to consent to receive Mildred James among us, for she is so conceited and overbearing that she is simply unendurable. Those that have gone astray we will let them be, for our duty is to try and keep others on the path of true and virtuous womanhood," argued Lillie.

"That's the way of the world, and the world is very hard and cold. Miss James belongs to the Christian Endeavor Society, and associates with the best of us in all church affairs. She is not wholly lost. The good in her may yet predominate over the evil. Anyhow, our interest in her will show that we are at least Christians trying to do, and to teach others to do what is right and womanly, for to be a lady one must be a be a modest woman."

"You are positively incorrigible, and there is another drawback also. After all we have said, it is possible that she may not wish to join us. You know a great number of our girls are very dark, and Mildred may simply reply by a pert 'declined with thanks', or something equally as impertinent," persisted Lillian.

"Oh well, that's quite a different aspect. I shall include her name, and if she declines to join us, then she must abide by the consequences, for mark me, Lillian, some day she will be sorry for her folly."

"And I for one will be downright glad to see the day that her proud spirit is humbled, for she is too overbearing for me."

"We all have our faults, my dear Lillie, and yours, I'm sorry to say, is impetuosity. You must try to check that impulsive manner of yours and be not quite so hasty in your judgment of others. Whatever you think or may say of an erring girl, remember that a great deal depends upon what sort of home influence one has had," said Laura impulsively but at that moment several girls came in and the conversation terminated abruptly.

Mildred James was truly a most beautiful girl. Her well developed figure was tall and graceful, and her complexion was exceedingly light. She possessed a wealth of luxuriant an rippling brown hair, and large, flashing brown eyes. She was also well-educated and fashionable, though decidedly supercilious. Her mother, a stout, yellow woman, had done all in her power to (using one of the old woman's phrases), "make a lady of Milly."

She had toiled early and late over the washtub and

ironing board, and so far as education and dress was concerned, she had not labored in vain. But in her efforts she had overlooked — or rather was ignorant of the minor things which helped to form the character of a lady.

Aunt Dolly (as the old lady was generally called) had petted and spoiled Mildred all her life, so when Mildred had expressed her disgust of all manual toil, her mother had given in to her, inwardly assuring herself that some day "Milly will be a great school teacher and take care of her ole ma." And while Aunt Dolly bent over tubs of streaming, foamy suds in the kitchen, dainty Mildred played the piano in the parlor, or attended numerous church entertainments and parties.

Consequently while she was growing from girlhood into womanhood, all girlish confidences and minor things such as every mother should share with her daughter were withheld from Aunt Dolly and Mildred became a haughty, conceited, overbearing creature, deeming even her mother far beneath her, as well as all others of darker hue. On account of her extreme whiteness of skin, she had obtained a position as typewriter in an Anglo-Saxon office, and many were the whispered comments bestowed upon her name. But whenever they were so unfortunate as to reach her ears, these whisperings only received a slight shrug of her dainty shoulders and a frown of silent contempt.

Being so very beautiful it is not necessary to mention the fact that she possessed many admirers. One of the most ardent was Robert Thompson, a rather handsome young man, though exceedingly dark, which last was with Mildred, his only drawback. On the same evening that Lillian Jones and Laura Claire were discussing the events which transpired in the first part of the story, Mildred was making her toilette preparatory to attending a school reception, when her mother called to tell her that Bob, Jinnie Thompson's boy, was in the sitting room to see her.

She had taken great pains with her toilette, and when she entered the parlor with her hair caught back in a loose coil down on her neck, and clad in a perfectly fitting gown of the palest pink satin and rich black velvet ribbons, Robert thought that he had never before seen such a lovely woman. And before he was aware of the fact he was at her side, telling her of his love for her and begging her to be his bride.

"My dear Robert, you must certainly be mad to carry on in this ridiculous fashion. Why, you have hardly said good evening yet." She said this in her most careless manner, at the same time motioning to him to be seated.

"Oh Mildred darling, pray don't jest with me. I was never more serious before in my life. I love you, Mildred."

"Stop right where you are, Bobby, for after I have talked this matter over with you and shown you how ridiculous you can be at times, you may regret saying so much. In the first place, you are poor as a church mouse, and you know that I must have money and plenty of it when I make up my mind to get married."

"I am not wealthy and that's a fact, but then I am on

the road to make money. Besides, I am going to be promoted to a higher office within a few weeks. My employer has just notified me, and the salary I'll receive will enable me to keep a wife in good circumstances. Oh Milly, think what you are saying. I love you well, and will try to make a good husband."

"It's no use, Bobby, we were not made for each other. I like you real well, but not well enough to trust my life with you. We should live miserably for I should be satisfied to do housework, and you certainly could not afford to keep a servant. I am sorry, but I will be a burden to you."

Although her countenance was quite serene, he could see that her eyes were mocking him.

"Great Scott, Mildred, this is no laughing matter. I am no boy to be jested with. I love you and asked you to be my wife and you make a fellow feel like a—"

"If you are going to swear about this matter, I'll leave the room until you are through."

"No. No, please don't go. Mildred darling, say that you will be mine," he pleaded.

"Whether I will or not?" she asked, jeeringly.

"Mildred, I am not playing with you. Answer. Will you be my wife?"

"No, I will not be your wife," she answered seriously now.

"Why won't you? I am sure you like me well enough; you led me on shamefully."

"Do you want me to tell you the reason why?"

"Certainly."

"You are sure you won't be angry?"

"I'll try not to be."

"Very well then, you are too dark, and you haven't got money enough," she replied, with her eyes on the carpet.

Robert did not start or make any outward show of his feelings, but the words stung him to the quick. He was still regarding her scarlet countenance with an expression of incredulity. The scales fell from his eyes. Her beauty faded and he saw only a cold, heartless woman of the world. Instantly the rumors he had heard concerning her situation returned to him. He had believed them false, but she had just told him that money with her was a necessary article. She must then be her employer's — impossible! Mildred James, whom he had thought so sweet, so good and pure this beautiful girl standing before him the mistress of some white man? Oh God, it could be true. She had almost confessed it.

"What's the matter, Bobby, are you angry? I love you."

"Enough, Miss James. Do not make me despise you. I understand, it is well — goodbye. Goodbye, and may God forgive you, for I cannot," he cried hoarsely as he reached for his hat and left the apartment.

He found his way out alone, and as he was descending the front steps a man hurried past him up them and pulled the bell vigorously. It was Lemuel P. Flemings, one of or rather, the favorite admirer of

Mildred. He had come to escort her to the reception.

Lemuel Flemings was a good looking man. Tall, very light, with jet black curls and a handsome black moustache. He was from up north, and was reputed to have lots of money. He had a smooth tongue and was a well-spoken young man, and therefore with the girls a 'great catch'.

Aunt Dolly did not like him and cautioned Mildred against him.

"This here Lem Flemin's, he comes from God knows where, filling all you young gals heads with a lot of nonsense and high perluting words 'til you nigh 'bout gone crazy over him. 'Deed I like that boy of Jinnie Thompson's a heap sight better an' I'm positive he'll make you the best husband if he is black. Black is honest, anyhow you knows more 'bout Bob than you do 'bout this Lem Flemin's."

But Mildred had flown into a passion, saying that Mr. Flemings was not only a gentleman, but wealthy accordingly. That she supposed she was free to marry whom she chose. And that if she married Mr. Flemings she would live like a lady, whereby if she married Bobby, she would probably break her back over the washtub and ironing board. But her mother had replied that "an old sheep knows the road and young lambs must learn the way," also "if you make your bed hard you must lie on it."

But nothing could move Mildred once she was bent on doing mischief, and she led him on as she had done many other young men with honest intentions.

But she had made up her mind to accept Lemuel and live in a whirl of gaiety and fashionable life as "That beautiful Mrs. Flemings," before whom all should bow.

So the engagement was announced on the same night that she had so coolly thrown Bobby over.

As Lillian Jones had predicted, Mildred had sent a dainty note to the club, 'declining with thanks', on a plea of being too busy with sundry social duties to find time to attend the meetings.

"I knew she would do this," exclaimed Lillie, as she and Laura were alone in the latter's sitting room.

"Poor girl, it's too bad; you see her mother has spoiled her to death, and she knows we have heard certain rumors, and how she threw poor Bobby over, so she thinks she will have no dealings with us whatever," said Laura, sympathizingly.

"It's a mighty good thing she didn't, for I am sure she would have been snubbed shamefully. And the way she is leading Flemings around is perfectly disgraceful."

"Oh, not so shameful after all; you know she is engaged to him. You are so unjust, Lillie," pleaded Laura.

"Oh, I am not so kind hearted as you are, Laura. You were even kind enough to pick poor Bobby up after she had thrown him over."

"Oh, Lillie."

"Now please don't think I meant that as a slur. What I mean is that you are trying to comfort him with your at all times true sympathy, but," and she stole a sly glance of Laura's face, "you are losing your heart in an attempt to mend Bobby's."

"Am I? Well, I confess I always did like Bobby, and he says that he doesn't think he really loved Mildred. He was simply blinded, and after what she confessed to him, he was glad that she wouldn't accept him."

"Oh, what did she confess to him?" asked Lillian, consumed with curiosity.

"Why, he would not tell me. He said that whatever it was it caused him to lose all respect for her," answered Laura.

So Mildred was married and left town for a two months' wedding trip, and when she returned the latest news afloat was that Robert Thompson and Laura Claire were engaged to be married. It surprised Mildred too, for she thought surely that Bobby would not get over his heartache for at least a year, and it was hardly six months before he was actually engaged to be married. She loved Bobby better than she did her husband, but thought to get over it with her husband's great wealth.

But when six months of married life had gone by, and operations on the great Flemings mansion — which had been rumored was to be erected — had not begun, people began to talk and to say that "Lem Flemings wasn't what he was cracked up to be," and " 'Deed Lem didn't have nothing nohow but education and high-perluting words." One old gossip went so far as to say that " 'Deed her old man often sees Lem coming outta Jayson's gambling rooms."

This was very true, for Lemuel was an inveterate gambler, and many were the nights that his beautiful young wife had waited his return in vain. This was a sore trial to Mildred, who had expected so much from this marriage, and when it became known that Robert Thompson had made a great deal of money of late and was building a beautiful house, she soon began to look faded and old.

At the end of one year of married life Milly found herself the mother of a bouncing baby boy, the arrival of which brought Lemuel to a sense of shame, and for three months he devoted himself to his wife and babe. But the novelty of this wore off after a while and he took to the old life again. And people began to whisper that "Lem Flemings wouldn't rest 'til he went to jail," and that "All of Milly's fine dresses and jewelry had been sold to pay Lem's gambling debts."

All of which was very true, and before Mildred had been married two years, she found herself a veritable slave, toiling like her mother before her, so that her sweet young child might have bread to eat, while Robert Thompson and his dashing young bride lived in a whirl of fashionable society.

BERNICE, THE OCTOROON
Mrs. Marie Louise Burgess-Ware

Learn to dissemble wrongs, to smile at injuries,
And suffer crimes thou wantst the power to punish
Be easy, affable, familiar, friendly
Search and know all mankind's mysterious ways,
But trust the secret of thy soul to none,
This is the way,
This only, to be safe in such a world as this is.
— Rowe's Ulysses

"I'll not grieve longer over what may never be. Sometimes I think my lot hard, cruel, and unjust, then I remember that others suffer as keenly, if not more, than I."

These words were spoken by a beautiful girl, scarcely out of her teens. Her evenly developed head was covered with golden curls that reminded me of burnished gold, as the rays of sunlight fell upon them.

Her blonde complexion, dainty mouth, and deep blue
eyes completed one of the loveliest faces.

She lifted her tear-stained face, so like a Madonna's,
filled with unutterable love. Rising, she exclaimed, "I
must attend to my duties. I want no traces of tears on
my face. Inquisitive little children may ask questions
that perhaps will make my heart bleed."

She bathed her swollen eyes, brushed back the curls
from her forehead, and rang the bell which told the
children recess was over. About forty little ones came
marching into the schoolroom, all sizes and ages, and of
every conceivable shade peculiar to the Negro race.
Such bright faces, sparkling eyes and pretty teeth.

"Miss Bernice," as they called her, seemed to have
good command of these little ones, although she
appeared to be of a gentle, yielding temperament.
Could you have looked into this country schoolhouse,
with its rough benches, ragged children and great
inconveniences, you would have wondered what this
college-bred lady was doing in the back woods of a
Southern State, when a teacher less tenderly reared
would have answered as well. Was it for money? Was it
love of the race? The latter was the reason. This cultured
octoroon, refined and fair as an Anglo-Saxon, was one
of a despised race, and had only recently learned it.

Bernice Silva was a native of Ohio. Her father, a man
of wealth and position, had married Pauline Blanchard
twenty years before this story opens. She was the
daughter of a wealthy Kentucky planter, and had been
educated in a Western College, together with her sister,

Mrs. Gadsden. The young couple were very happy, and when Bernice came with her wealth of golden curls, she was called 'papa's sunbeam' by the delighted young father, whose life she crowned with joy.

All that wealth could bestow was lavished upon this child, and at a proper age, she, too, was sent to college. She became a great favorite with teachers and classmates, because of her winsome disposition and brilliant gifts as a student, her musical talent being of a very high order.

Mrs. Gadsden had a daughter Lenore who was also at college with Bernice. The two cousins were exact opposites in all things — Lenore was as dark as Bernice was fair, as envious as Bernice was generous, she had a heart filled with jealousy and hatred for her beautiful cousin. Beautiful herself, her haughtiness repelled those who aspired to her friendship. This was more the result of over-indulgence, for after Mr. Gadsden's death, the child was given her own will in all things.

The winter after the girls were graduated was spent by both families in the picturesque town of St. Augustine, Florida. Society there was made up of many Northern and Southern aristocrats, who greeted with open arms two beautiful and accomplished young women, possessed of wealth and prestige. There was a flutter of expectancy throughout the little colony when cards were issued for a reception on Thanksgiving evening by Mrs. Silva, and the fortunate recipients counted themselves very lucky.

It was a night long remembered in St. Augustine. The

spacious rooms were crowded by brave men and fair
women. Flowers filled the air with fragrance, birds sang
in gilded cages, fountains played, their perfumed
waters falling in prismatic shades under constantly
changing colored electrical lights; the dreamy, pulsating
notes of the band were a welcome accompaniment to
romantic conversation.

It was a memorable reception for all, but for Garrett
Purnello life took a sudden change. The promising
young barrister never again had eyes for a woman's fair
face. He was much impressed by Bernice's beauty and
modesty. He, with his passionate Spanish blood, loved
her then and forever. She, with her pure heart returned
his love unconsciously.

Several days later, Bernice saw her father coming
towards the house, accompanied by Mr. Purnello. They
came immediately to the drawing room where Mrs.
Silva and her daughter were sitting. After the usual
greetings, Mr. Silva said, "I brought Mr. Purnello home
to lunch, and we have been having a lively discussion of
the race question. This recent disfranchisement, and the
attitude taken by the majority of our sound citizens
towards the black men of this country, appears unjust to
me. To be sure, the ignorant vote of any people is not fit
to be counted, but still the Negro excites my pity.
Ushered out of slavery into an unknown sphere of life,
many have made themselves worthy to bear the name
of citizen. And wholesale disfranchisement is to rob him
almost of life itself. One wonders if mob law is not a
stigma on our beloved republic; this sweet land of

liberty, the land of the noble free. It is as if the fatherhood of God and the brotherhood of man existed only in legends of Holy Writ. Peaceful black citizens are driven from their homes because a mob decides that they must leave a community. Is there no panacea for this evil, for evil it is?"

"To my mind, there is but one remedy," replied the younger man, "and that is being applied by Booker T. Washington and other advocates of Industrial Education. The masses of the blacks and the poor whites of our Southland must be educated, not only in books, but in trades and all those other things which crush out idleness and keep down vice. If we consider the matter seriously, we find that all this disturbance arises between the poor whites and the illiterate blacks. The intelligent Negro does not clamor for social equality, he is satisfied to be a leader of his people."

"What you say is true," replied Mr. Silva, "but it is an outrage to know that men are driven from their homes because they are Negroes. Debarred from all things which protect the white laborer, yet in spite of all this, they multiply and grow in mental and physical strength. Like the Jews they are favored of God, although despised by men. But this is dull conversation for the ladies; we will change the subject."

"But, papa," exclaimed Bernice, "I have read much concerning this matter; do not discontinue the conversation because mamma and I are here. I am sure that what involves the welfare of our country is interesting to us, and must be to all true women."

Garrett listened eagerly; it was rare to find so sweet a girl and one so young, finding attraction in words of wisdom and discretion. A pleasant hour was spent about the social board, and then the two gentlemen spent another enjoyable hour in the music room. Garrett was entranced by the wonderful gifts possessed by Bernice. Thus sped many pleasant days, merging into weeks, and it was soon plain to the onlooking world that the young people loved each other. It was the old, old story, ever fresh, ever new.

Lenore looked on with a heart swelling with envy and indignation. She was beautiful too; why was it that the only man she had ever felt she could love, found no attraction in her? That Bernice should take him from her filled her heart with most bitter thoughts. She clinched her hands in rage as she walked the floor of her room, and swore to part them.

Very soon the engagement of these popular young people was announced. Mr. Silva reluctantly consented to give his treasure to Garrett. All his affection was centered on this beautiful child, and he could not bear to think of trusting her happiness in a stranger's hands; but he smiled as he said to his wife:

"Thus it is our daughters leave us, those we love and those who love us."

About six weeks after the betrothal, Mrs. Purnello and Garrett took tea with Bernice. Mr. and Mrs. Silva had taken a trip to Tuskegee Institute. They had given considerable money for the education of the Freedmen, and so wished to see this school of schools. Mrs. Gadsden was acting hostess, and had planned a very pretty tea. Lenore had changed greatly during the past few weeks, and everyone attributed it to ill-health. In spite of this, she tried to assume her usual manner.

While they were enjoying the tea an old Negro servant came into the room, with some tea cakes which had been forgotten. Bernice smiled at her, and admired the pretty bandana 'kerchief which she wore.

Mrs. Purnello, with a scornful smile, said quickly, "Bernice, don't admire these Negroes; they get beside themselves. I despise them. If it were not for their labor, I would be glad to have them swept out of existence."

Bernice was startled at such language from a lady's lips. Garrett was mortified; he knew his mother hated Negroes, and was oftentimes very eccentric about them. But such an outburst startled him.

Bernice glanced at Mrs. Purnello and said, "You surely could not have had a good old mammy for your nurse. Why not let these people live and thrive? We are taught, and pretend to believe that God created all alike; that Christ died for all, and commands us as Christians to love our fellow man. We are taught next to our duty to God, to love our neighbor as ourselves. How can you entertain such a feeling in your bosom, and be a member of Christ's Church?"

"Lawd, honey, you're a Christian. Don't you waste your breath, she ain't got no religion of any kind. My sole this minute is heaps whiter'n her face," and the old woman shrugged her shoulders, and withdrew from the dining room.

Bernice looked pained. She was about to say something, when Mrs. Purnello said in her haughtiest manner, "Bernice, we will not discuss this subject further; you must relinquish some of your strange ideas about this matter. My son's future wife cannot hold such views. You have much to learn; I hope never to hear such expressions again in my presence."

"But, my dear madam, I have no desire to lay aside my good breeding nor my own convictions. I can never learn to be cruel to a race of people who have never injured me. We have become rich through their toil. Their faults have not blinded me to their nobler qualities. They have hearts as tender as my own. All my life my heart has gone out to them, and when my parents have received appeals for help from their various homes and institutions of learning, I have longed to help them myself in some way."

Lenore had sat a silent spectator of the scene. Now she spoke.

"You can have your wish; nothing is easier, for you are one of them. Do you not know your mother is of Negro ancestry?"

For a moment dead silence followed her words. Bernice turned white to the lips. Garrett overcame his first anger and consternation with a laugh. He had seen through Lenore's jealousy for some time. But Mrs. Purnello held up both hands in horror. She moved away from Bernice, as if the air were contaminated.

Recovering herself by a great effort, Bernice smiled. She was not now the little girl whom everyone thought so meek and gentle; her eyes sparkled, her air breathed defiance.

"How long have you known this, Lenore?"

"My parents have always known it," replied Lenore, now somewhat frightened at what she had done.

"Then, if one drop of that despised blood flows in my veins, loyal to that race I will be. I did not expect such a blow from you, Lenore."

The latter made no reply, but left the room, apparently satisfied with the mischief done.

"Garrett," said Mrs. Purnello, greatly agitated, "Bernice cannot expect you to fulfill your engagement under these unfortunate conditions. You cannot marry a Negro."

Garrett had been silent all through the storm aroused by Lenore's assertion. He faced his mother with unusual sternness on his handsome face.

"Mother, you have said enough; if you have no respect for us, have a little for yourself. Do not hide all that is womanly in you. Remember, Bernice is a woman, and has a woman's tender feelings, and it is not necessary to try to crush her. She is dearer to me than ever, because if she be really a negro, she will need me more than ever. She may be good and pure, but she will be counted by many as no better than the most common type of her race. I will stand by her until death. I see in her all that is pure and lovely in woman. I love her with a love devoid of prejudice; it is too late for that to separate us."

"Then you are no longer my son."

"As you say, mother. A man's word is his bond. I am strong; she is weak. I will protect her. I am willing to give up even you, because you are wrong. Where is the warm feeling which should fill your bosom as a woman? I fear, mother, there is a touch of something unnatural and inhuman in your conduct."

"Bernice, let me appeal to you. Garrett is unreasonable and Quixotic. After the first few months of married life, he would become dissatisfied and unhappy. But if you will keep this matter secret, perhaps we can hide it from the world; but if you persist in allying your fortunes with Negroes, then our friendship must end. I love Garrett; I would like to see him happy, but I love my good name too well to wish him to marry into an alien race. As you value your future happiness, think well before you decide."

Bernice smiled.

"My dear Mrs. Purnello, I see no difference between you and me; my tastes are as refined and cultured as yours. My skin is fairer than many of our acquaintances. My parents as cultured. Why should I be persecuted because mamma is of mixed origin? Did not God create all in His own image? Are we not taught that He is the father of all mankind? Because the despised blood of the Negro chances to flow through my veins, must I be trampled upon and persecuted? Let me ask you, how did it happen that your ancestors, whom you claim were so chivalrous and aristocratic stooped to mix with an inferior race, and thus flood the country with the mulattoes, quadroons, and octoroons that are so bitterly despised by many of both races? Well may you blush when you think of such chivalry. My heart warms to the inferior race, and I will give all that I have in learning and culture, to follow in the footsteps of the great Teacher who said, 'Inasmuch as ye have done it unto the least of these my brethren, ye have done it unto me'."

Mrs. Purnello left the room without replying to Bernice.

Turning to Bernice, Garrett exclaimed passionately, "Think, Bernice, all that this means. Can you stand the snubs, insults and temptations? My dear girl, you know not what you will have to encounter. Many will think you an Anglo-Saxon, and will treat you kindly, but if they find out what you really are, there is no ignorant Negro who will be treated more contemptuously. I cannot bear to think of it. Marry me, and forget all that has just happened."

"Garrett, I appreciate your kind thoughts for my welfare. I could not agree to anything but the right. Were I to accept your proposition I would feel like a woman wearing a mask. There is too much at stake. The sins of the fathers are surely visited upon the children. The Negro blood would show itself, if not in my children, in some of the coming generations. The so-called curse will follow us, and I would not blight your life. I know I have been beyond recognition all these years; others have been and others will be," replied Bernice sadly.

"I admire and love you more than ever; do not come to a hasty conclusion, even though you are right; you must not injure yourself. Talk with your parents, be guided by them; tomorrow we may be better able to decide what is best to be done under the circumstances. You are mine; I will never give you up this side of eternity."

He was sincere; this was no passing fancy. He loved her. He began to wonder why the white man should be the dominant race, and considered so far above his educated negro brother. In his heart, he thought it unjust. He was sorely perplexed in spirit. He thought of the passage of Scripture, 'God is no respecter of persons', and wondered what it meant. His own sorrow was not to be compared with his sympathy for Bernice. When he thought of what she had been subjected to, the muscles of his face became rigid, the veins became prominent; his countenance showed the great anguish through which he was passing.

When Mr. Silva learned of the unwomanly conduct of Lenore, he was shocked; first of all, because of her treachery; secondly, because of the Negro blood in his wife's veins. It was true that Mrs. Silva and Mrs. Gadsden were only half-sisters. They were originally from Kentucky. Their father, Joseph Blanchard, had been a wealthy slave owner. He had educated them at the same college, and when, by accident, Beatrice had learned that Pauline's mother was her 'mammy', she was too horrified to expose it. She loved her sister, and as the world was none the wiser, it was quietly covered up, and both daughters married well. Had Garrett Purnello loved Lenore, this story would never have been written.

Mr. and Mrs. Silva were grieved for Bernice. They cared nothing for themselves, but to have her life clouded in its springtime caused them much pain. They knew they could return to their Western home unmolested. But Bernice was determined not to sail under false colors, and had made up her mind to teach her people. She had a deep sense of right and wrong, and then, knowing the depth of the chasm existing between the two races, was not willing to remain in a false position. She knew nothing of her people, their manners and customs, nor the hardships which many had to endure. She did not dream of the discouragements awaiting her. She saw only their needs and her ability to help them. The ragged, ignorant, or unclean of either race, she had never come in contact with. She was ignorant of the vice that existed in the world; you can imagine her consternation at the sights she saw.

After much persuasion, her parents consented to let her go to Maryland to teach a parish school. When our story opens she is in the schoolroom, trying to teach forty mischievous little children.

"Sit down my dear," Bernice said, pointing to a little picanniny as black as midnight. Her head was covered with short, knotty hair, that looked as if a comb had never passed through it.

What a name for such a looking child. 'Fairlily'. She

wondered where the mother got the name. Then there
was a little boy named Esther. He had an unusually
large head and beautiful black eyes. His body was small
and badly nourished, and the little creature seemed to
have what is known as the rickets. The next one that
attracted her attention was as white as the others were
black. Her face was freckled, her hair sandy and stringy.
She looked very much out of place. Looking about her,
Bernice noticed similar children scattered here and
there. She thought this the most motley crowd she had
ever seen; there were no two alike.

"And these are my people," she mused, "indeed it is
a mixture. Where did they come from, and how did they
become like this?"

It never entered her pure mind that many of these
knew no father; it did not dawn upon her that a race
despising hers was at every opportunity flooding the
country with children born to be despised and
persecuted. Some of these little ones were ragged and
hungry, whose fathers lived luxury, while their mothers
were ignorant women who knew nothing of the
development of their intellectual being, but allowed
their animal natures to predominate, and brought forth
children regardless of the laws of God or man, and thus
these poor children's opportunities to become noble
men and women were very limited.

Bernice was the picture of a modern Priscilla in her
simple black gown, white cuffs and apron. Her eyes
were red from excessive weeping, her heart cried out in
its loneliness, her task was very hard. Her boarding

place was unlike her comfortable home. The log cabin had only three rooms, two of which were unfinished. Her room was the best in the house, and had a clean, bare floor, an old-fashioned bed covered with brilliantly colored quilts of various designs, a strip of home-made rag carpet answered for a mat, and two pine chairs and a table. The people around her were very sensitive, and she had to guard against hurting anyone's feelings, for they soon would brand her as an "educated and stuck-up yaller nigger." The food was coarse, the greens, which she ate very often, were a new article of food to her; the corn pones seemed heavy; the biscuits were a sore trial to her digestive organs, for she was used to home-made, light bread, and had never eaten very many biscuits. She had longed for a porterhouse steak, broiled and juicy, but that was unheard-of fare.

In spite of the many disadvantages, she labored on, teaching a Sabbath School in connection with her other work. It pleased her to see the children eagerly listening to the story she told them about the first Christmas. One little fellow with bright eyes, said, "Lawd, Miss Bernice, I never knew Christmas meant a thing more'n hanging up you stockings and gittin presents. No one ever told us anything else. Why, we gits up and runs across to Aunt Nancy and hollers, 'Christmas Gift'. She grins and says, 'You the same, honey', and we all has a big time Ma comes home from the white folks, and then we I hear the chickens holler, and the eggs a beating, and Miss Nicey, you can smell the egg nog way down the road. I can taste the pound cake right now."

Bernice smiled. She thought that there was no need
of going to Africa to do missionary work, there was
plenty right here. Her sewing school was enjoyed not
only by the little girls, but their mothers came also. One
day each week she taught them how to cook and
prepare food for the table in a scientific manner. Such
poverty, ignorance and superstition as she saw among
the lowest types. Christian education was badly needed
to save both soul and body. The public schools kept
open only three or four months during the year, then to
the pea-picking and other farming. Parents barely
received money enough to provide for their large
families, and the people were types of illiteracy. There
were many strange customs which Bernice had never
heard of, such as wakes. When the people died, in the
dead hours of the night you would hear wild shrieks go
up in the air, which would make you shudder, and then
again you would hear a weird melody followed by a
loud prayer over the dead. Everyone at the wakes did
not partake of the spirits which always were there, but
enough drank of it to give much to the occasion.

The spiritual condition was bad; preachers were
almost always called of God, but not very often
educated and fitted for the work. The preacher was
judged by the strength of his preachings, and oftentimes
the number of big words which he used. A revival
meant great excitement, exhortations and much hilarity.
Mourners went to the mourners' bench under the heat
of a sermon which had a vividly painted picture of a
burning lake, and his satanic majesty and his host

standing ready with their cloven feet and pitchforks to throw the victims into the lake before them. People no mourned often, wrestled for several days before Satan would leave their bodies, and when they felt him as he parted, they arose and made known their experiences to the remaining sinners.

Many might have thought this ludicrous, but Bernice thought it a sad sight in a Christian land. The Negroes whom she had seen during her life were not of this type; they were people whom education and Christianity had made intelligent men and women. She felt certain that religion scared into a person could not last after the excitement was over, and how she longed to instill into the little hearts under her control that God's Holy Word and His Spirit would make them better, if they would quietly ask Him, and make up their little minds to do His will.

This town was twenty miles from any railroads, hence its backwardness.

Bernice had imported an organ. The little voices were so sweet and mellow, she often likened them to the mocking birds which warbled before her school door. Many of the people had never seen or heard an organ. How they did enjoy the music. It was not long before she learned to accompany their beautiful plantation melodies, although to a listener they are much sweeter without an instrument.

There was an interesting old lady who never missed a Sabbath. She led the melodies, and the children joined in with much fervor. Bernice could not help being touched by the weird tones and the soul-stirring words.

One Sabbath morning there was a funeral, and dear Aunt Martha led the music at the graveyard. They had all assembled around the grave; the air was filled with unearthly shrieks, the mourners were determined that everybody should know they were bereaved. Even in the midst of all the sorrow, there was something most amusing. One of the mourners had a red bandana handkerchief, wiping her eyes under a heavy crape veil. The minister committed the body to the ground with a voice loud and trembling. Old Aunt Martha raised her voice:

> *Mother an father, pray for me*
> *Mother and father, pray for me*
> *Mother and father, pray for me*
> *I've got a home in Galilee.*

> *CHORUS*
> *Can't you live humble?*
> *Praise King Jesus*
> *Can't you live humble?*
> *Dying Lamb.*

The mourners wailed, the brothers shouted. Such a scene. Bernice had never witnessed the like before nor since. She looked towards her friend, Aunt Martha. Great drops of perspiration were rolling off her face, the tears were streaming down her cheeks, as she sang:

When you hear my coffin sound
When you hear my coffin sound
When you hear my coffin sound
You may know I've gone around.

There stood the old lady, under the shade of the trees, singing with all her might. Eighty-one years old, the mother Of twenty-one children, unlettered, but trilling like a bird.

Bernice was an earnest Christian, she believed above all things in the preservation of the purity of womanhood. She wanted to make every woman the highest type of truth, beauty, and goodness. The scenes which she witnessed in her new surroundings were strange to her, and yet they were real. What had she known of temptation — she who had been surrounded by all that was pure and lovely, whose moral and religious training had been of the highest order? She was unacquainted with the ways of the outside world; her life had been lived among those whose every thought had been for her and of her. She knew nothing of the life of the lowly, of the sin which surrounded them everywhere, of the temptations which they resisted as well as yielded to. In her weak way she tried to reach the hearts of the women to teach them by her example, as well as by talks in her mothers' meetings, that if they overcame temptation and repented of their sins then would come real strength of character and true religion.

She had heard lectures by people engaged in work among the black men. She had thought that much of the degradation and ignorance mentioned was exaggeration. She was entirely unprepared for the scenes which she encountered. Superstition prevailed. There were signs for everything:

The guinea hens could not 'holler' unless fallen weather

was sure to follow.

An owl could not hoot in the tree before the house unless

it must be followed by a death in that family.

The rooster could not crow before the door unless hasty

news followed, and if he dared to strut away from the

door and crow as he was leaving what would be the

result? Why, the news of a death would soon reach the

family.

The dog must not howl, if so, the neighborhood all

wondered to whom this death warning had been sent.

These are only a very few of the many strange signs Bernice listened to.

She visited the homes of the children, and when sickness came it was she who knew just what to do for them, and how to do it. She showed the old people many things that they might do for the comfort of their suffering ones. She spent many nights by the bedsides of the sick ones; she prayed for them, comforted those who mourned, and in numerous ways brought sunshine into the homes.

There was one old mammy, Aunt Lizzie, by name. She was one of those tall, well-built Negro women of pure blood, perfect in physique, and handsome in features. Her black skin was as smooth as satin, her teeth like pearl. She had a little daughter wasting away with consumption. Nor was it to be wondered at, for they lived in a two-room house, unfit for renting. They were a family of nine. Tina was the oldest. The parents were what is known as 'hardshell Baptists'. They believed in foot-washing, and many other strange things known only to that set of Baptists. When Bernice came to care for her pupil, they looked on in wonder. Their place was very humble; it boasted of two beds in the front room and one in the kitchen. On one of the beds in the front room Tina lay, on the brink of eternity. The mother was washing, trying to obtain the means to provide extra comforts for Tina, the father working hard to earn the regular support, four dollars a week. Bernice made the room tidy, bathed the feverish child, and made her little delicacies. Tina grasped Bernice's hands as she lay dying, and exclaimed, "Oh, Miss Bernice, you've done told me 'bout heaven, Jesus and the angels; tell Mammy too." And with Bernice's hands on her burning brow the child's spirit went into Paradise.

Bernice helped prepare her for burial, and if you can picture the family in its poverty and sorrow, the pine coffin, costing the paltry sum of seven dollars, the golden-rod and flowers which covered the coffin that contained the loving mother's child, you would feel that it is only too true that one half of the world knows not how the other half lives. The love in that ignorant yet tender heart would put to shame some of our more intelligent mothers.

TALMA GORDON
Pauline E. Hopkins

The Canterbury Club of Boston was holding its regular monthly meeting at the palatial Beacon Street residence of Dr. William Thornton, expert medical practitioner and specialist. All the members were present, because some rare opinions were to be aired by men of profound thought on a question of vital importance to the life of the Republic, and because the club celebrated its anniversary in a home usually closed to society. The Doctor's winters, since his marriage, were passed at his summer home near his celebrated sanatorium. This winter found him in town with his wife and two boys. We had heard much of the beauty of the former, who was entirely unknown to social life, and about whose life and marriage we felt sure a romantic interest attached. The Doctor himself was too bright a luminary of the professional world to remain long hidden without creating comment. We had accepted the invitation to dine with alacrity, knowing that we should be welcomed to a banquet that would feast both eye and palate; but we had not been favored by even a glimpse of the hostess. The subject for discussion was: *Expansion; Its Effect upon the Future Development of the Anglo-Saxon throughout the World.*

Dinner was over, but we still sat about the social board, discussing the question of the hour. The Hon. Herbert Clapp, eminent jurist and politician, had painted in glowing colors the advantages to be gained by the increase of wealth and the exalted position which expansion would give the United States in the councils of the great governments of the world. In smoothly flowing sentences marshalled in rhetorical order with compact ideas and incisive argument, he drew an effective picture with all the persuasive eloquence of the trained orator.

Joseph Whitman, the theologian of worldwide fame accepted the arguments of Mr. Clapp, but subordinated all to the great opportunity which expansion would give to the religious enthusiast. None could doubt the sincerity of this man, who looked once into the idealised face on which heaven had set the seal of consecration.

Various opinions were advanced by the twenty-five men present, but the host said nothing; he glanced from one to another with a look of amusement in his shrewd gray-blue eyes. "Wonderful eyes," said his patients who came under their magic spell. "A wonderful man and a wonderful mind," agreed his contemporaries, as they heard in amazement of some great cure of chronic or malignant disease which approached the supernatural.

"What do you think of this question, Doctor?" finally asked the president, turning to the silent host.

"Your arguments are good; they would convince almost anyone."

"But not Doctor Thornton," laughed the theologian.

"I acquiesce which ever way the result turns. Still, I like to view both sides of a question. We have considered but one tonight. Did you ever think that in spite of our prejudices against amalgamation, some of our descendants, indeed many of them, will inevitably intermarry among those far-off tribes of dark-skinned peoples, if they become a part of this great Union ?"

"Among the lower classes that may occur, but not to any great extent," remarked a college president.

"My experience teaches me that it will occur among all classes, and to an appaling extent," replied the Doctor.

"You don't believe in intermarriage with other races?"

"Yes, most emphatically, when they possess decent moral development and physical perfection, for then we develop a superior being in the progeny born of the intermarriage. But if we are not ready to receive and assimilate the new material which will be brought to mingle with our pure Anglo-Saxon stream, we should call a halt in our expansion policy."

"I must confess, Doctor, that in the idea of amalgamation you present a new thought to my mind. Will you not favor us with a few of your main points?"

asked the president of the club, breaking the silence which followed the Doctor's remarks.

"Yes, Doctor, give us your theories on the subject. We may not agree with you, but we are all open to conviction."

The Doctor removed the half-consumed cigar from his lips, drank what remained in his glass of the choice Burgundy, and leaning back in his chair contemplated the earnest faces. Then he began his story:

We may make laws, but laws are but straws in the hands of Omnipotence. There's a divinity that shapes our ends, rough-hew them how we will. And no man may combat fate. Given a man, propinquity, opportunity, fascinating femininity, and there you are. Black, white, green, yellow — nothing will prevent intermarriage. Position, wealth, family, friends — all sink into insignificance before the God-implanted instinct that made Adam, awakening from a deep sleep and finding the woman beside him, accept Eve as bone of his bone; he cared not nor questioned whence she came. So it is with the sons of Adam ever since, through the law of heredity which makes us all one common family. And so it will be with us in our reformation of this old Republic. Perhaps I can make my meaning clearer by illustration, and with your permission I will tell you a story which came under my observation as a practitioner.

Doubtless all of you heard of the terrible tragedy which occurred at Gordonville, Mass., some years ago, when Capt. Jonathan Gordon, his wife and little son were murdered. I suppose that I am the only man on this side the Atlantic, outside of the police, who can tell you the true story of that crime.

I knew Captain Gordon well; it was through his persuasions that I bought a place in Gordonville and settled down to spending my summers in that charming rural neighborhood. I had rendered the Captain what he was pleased to call valuable medical help, and I became his family physician. Captain Gordon was a retired sea captain, formerly engaged in the East India trade. All his ancestors had been such; but when the bottom fell out of that business he established the Gordonville Mills with his first wife's money, and settled down as a money-making manufacturer of cotton cloth. The Gordons were old New England Puritans who had come over on the *Mayflower;* they had owned Gordon Hall for more than a hundred years. It was a baronial-like pile of granite with towers, standing on a hill which commanded a superb view of Massachusetts Bay and the surrounding country. I imagine the Gordon star was under a cloud about the time Captain Jonathan married his first wife, Miss Isabel Franklin of Boston, who brought to him the money which mended the broken fortunes of the Gordon house, and restored this old Puritan stock to its rightful position. In the person of Captain Gordon the austerity of manner and indomitable will-power that he had inherited were combined with a temper that brooked no contradiction.

The first wife died at the birth of her third child,

leaving him two daughters, Jeannette and Talma. Very soon after her death the Captain married again. I have heard it rumored that the Gordon girls did not get on very well with their stepmother. She was a woman with no fortune of her own, and envied the large portion left by the first Mrs. Gordon to her daughters.

Jeannette was tall, dark, and stern like her father; Talma was like her dead mother, and possessed of great talent, so great that her father sent her to the American Academy at Rome, to develop the gift. It was the hottest of July days when her friends were invited to an afternoon party on the lawn and a dance in the evening, to welcome Talma Gordon among them again. I watched her as she moved about among her guests, a fairylike blonde in floating white draperies, her face a study in delicate changing tints, like the heart of a flower, sparkling in smiles about the mouth to end in merry laughter in the clear blue eyes. There were all the subtle allurements of birth, wealth and culture about the exquisite creature:

> Smiling, frowning evermore,
> Thou art perfect in lovelore,
> Ever varying Madeline

quoted a celebrated writer as he stood apart with me, gazing upon the scene before us. He sighed as he looked at the girl.

"Doctor, there is genius and passion in her face. Sometime our little friend will do wonderful things. But is it desirable to be singled out for special blessings by the gods? Genius always carries with it intense capacity for suffering: 'Whom the gods love die young'."

"Ah," I replied, "do not name death and Talma Gordon together. Cease your dismal croakings; such talk is rank heresy."

The dazzling daylight dropped slowly into summer twilight. The merriment continued. More guests arrived; the great dancing pagoda built for the occasion was lighted by myriads of Japanese lanterns. The strains from the band grew sweeter and sweeter, and all went merry as a marriage bell. It was a rare treat to have this party at Gordon Hall, for Captain Jonathan was not given to hospitality. We broke up shortly before midnight, with expressions of delight from all the guests.

I was a bachelor then, without ties. Captain Gordon insisted upon my having a bed at the Hall. I did not fall asleep readily; there seemed to be something in the air that forbade it. I was still awake when a distant clock struck the second hour of the morning. Suddenly the heavens were lighted by a sheet of ghastly light; a terrific midsummer thunderstorm was breaking over the sleeping town. A lurid flash lit up all the landscape, painting the trees in grotesque shapes against the murky sky, and defining clearly the sullen blackness of the waters of the bay breaking in grandeur against the rocky coast. I had arisen and put back the draperies from the windows, to have an unobstructed view of the grand scene. A low muttering coming nearer and nearer, a terrific roar, and then a tremendous downpour. The storm had burst.

Now the uncanny howling of a dog mingled with the rattling volleys of thunder. I heard the opening and closing of doors; the servants were about looking after things. It was impossible to sleep. The lightning was more vivid. There was a blinding flash of a greenish-white tinge mingled with the crash of falling timbers. Then before my startled gaze arose columns of red flames reflected against the sky.

"Heaven help us," I cried. "It is the left tower; it has been struck and is on fire."

I hurried on my clothes and stepped into the corridor; the girls were there before me. Jeannette came up to me instantly with anxious face.

"Oh, Doctor Thornton, what shall we do? Papa and mamma and little Johnny are in the old left tower. It is on fire. I have knocked and knocked, but get no answer."

"Don't be alarmed," said I soothingly. "Jenkins, ring the alarm bell," I continued, turning to the butler who was standing near. "The rest follow me. We will force the entrance to the Captain's room."

Instantly, it seemed to me, the bell boomed out upon the now silent air, for the storm had died down as quickly as it arose; and as our little procession paused before the entrance to the old left tower, we could distinguish the sound of the fire engines already on their way from the village.

The door resisted all our efforts; there seemed to be a barrier against it which nothing could move. The flames were gaining headway. Still the same deathly silence within the rooms.

"Oh, will they never get here?" cried Talma, ringing her hands in terror. Jeannette said nothing, but her face was ashen. The servants were huddled together in a panic-stricken group. I can never tell you what a relief it was when we heard the first sound of the firemen's voices, saw their quick movements, and heard the ringing of the axes with which they cut away every obstacle to our entrance to the rooms. The neighbors who had just enjoyed the hospitality of the house were now gathered around offering all the assistance in their power. In less than fifteen minutes the fire was out, and the men began to bear the unconscious inmates from the ruins. They carried them to the pagoda so lately the scene of mirth and pleasure, and I took up my station there, ready to assume my professional duties. The Captain was nearest me; and as I stooped to make the necessary examination I reeled away from the ghastly sight which confronted me — Gentlemen, across the Captain's throat was a deep gash that severed the jugular vein.

The Doctor paused, and the hand with which he refilled his glass trembled violently.

"What is it, Doctor?" cried the men, gathering about me.

"Take the women away, this is murder."

"Murder," cried Jeannette, as she fell against the side of the pagoda.

"Murder," screamed Talma, staring at me as if unable

to grasp my meaning.

I continued my examination of the bodies, and found that the same thing had happened to Mrs. Gordon and to little Johnny.

The police were notified; and when the sun rose over the dripping town he found them in charge of Gordon Hall, the servants standing in excited knots talking over the crime, the friends of the family confounded, and the two girls trying to comfort each other and realise the terrible misfortune that had overtaken them.

Nothing in the rooms of the left tower seemed to have been disturbed. The door of communication between the rooms of the husband and wife was open, as they had arranged it for the night. Little Johnny's crib was placed beside his mother's bed. In it he was found as though never awakened by the storm. It was quite evident that the assassin was no common ruffian. The chief gave strict orders for a watch to be kept on all strangers or suspicious characters who were seen in the neighborhood. He made inquiries among the servants, seeing each one separately, but there was nothing gained from them. No one had heard anything suspicious; all had been awakened by the storm. The chief was puzzled. Here was a triple crime for which no motive could be assigned.

"What do you think of it?" I asked him, as we stood together on the lawn.

"It is my opinion that the deed was committed by one of the higher classes, which makes the mystery more difficult to solve. I tell you, Doctor, there are mysteries that never come to light, and this, I think, is one of them."

While we were talking, Jenkins, the butler, an old and trusted servant, came up to the chief and saluted respectfully.

"Want to speak with me, Jenkins?" he asked.

The man nodded, and they walked away together.

The story of the inquest was short, but appaling. It was shown that Talma had been allowed to go abroad to study because she and Mrs. Gordon did not get on well together. From the testimony of Jenkins it seemed that Talma and her father had quarrelled bitterly about her lover, a young artist whom she had met at Rome, who was unknown to fame, and very poor. There had been terrible things said by each, and threats even had passed, all of which now rose up in judgment against the unhappy girl. The examination of the family solicitor revealed the fact that Captain Gordon intended to leave his daughters only a small annuity the bulk of the fortune going to his son Jonathan, junior. This was a monstrous injustice, as everyone felt. In vain Talma protested her innocence. Someone must have done it. No one would be benefited so much by these deaths as she and her sister. Moreover, the will, together with other papers, was nowhere to be found. Not the slightest clue bearing upon the disturbing elements in this family, if any there were, was to be found.

As the only surviving relatives, Jeannette and Talma became joint heirs to an immense fortune, which only for the bloody tragedy just enacted would, in all probability, have passed them by. Here was the motive. The case was very black against Talma. The foreman stood up. The silence was intense.

"We find that Capt. Jonathan Gordon, Mary E. Gordon and Jonathan Gordon, junior, all deceased, came to their deaths by means of a knife or other sharp instrument in the hands of Talma Gordon."

The girl was like one stricken with death. The flower-like mouth was drawn and pinched; the great sapphire-blue eyes were black with passionate anguish, terror and despair. She was placed in jail to await her trial at the fall session of the criminal court. The excitement in the hitherto quiet town rose to fever pitch. Many points in the evidence seemed incomplete to thinking men. The weapon could not be found, nor could it be divined what had become of it. No reason could be given for the murder except the quarrel between Talma and her father and the ill-will which existed between the girl and her stepmother.

When the trial was called Jeannette sat beside Talma in the prisoner's dock; both were arrayed in deepest mourning. Talma was pale and care-worn, but seemed uplifted, spiritualised, as it were. Upon Jeannette the full realisation of her sister's peril seemed to weigh heavily. She had changed much too: hollow cheeks, tottering steps, eyes blazing with fever, all suggestive of rapid and premature decay. From far-off Italy Edward Turner, growing famous in the art world, came to stand beside his love in this hour of anguish.

The trial was a memorable one. No additional

evidence had been collected to strengthen the prosecution; when the attorney-general rose to open the case against Talma he knew, as everyone else did, that he could not convict solely on the evidence adduced. What was given did not always bear upon the case, and brought out strange stories of Captain Jonathan's methods. Tales were told of sailors who had sworn to take his life, in revenge for injuries inflicted upon them by his hand. One or two clues were followed, but without avail. The judge summed up the evidence impartially, giving the prisoner the benefit of the doubt. The points in hand furnished valuable collateral evidence, but were not direct proof. Although the moral presumption was against the prisoner, legal evidence was lacking to actually convict.

The jury found the prisoner 'Not Guilty', owing to the fact that the evidence was entirely circumstantial. The verdict was received in painful silence; then a murmur of discontent ran through the great crowd.

"She must have done it," said one, "who else has been benefited by the horrible deed?"

"A poor woman would not have fared so well at the hands of the jury, nor a homely one either, for that matter," said another.

The great Gordon trial was ended. Innocent or guilty, Talma Gordon could not be tried again. She was free, but her liberty, with blasted prospects and fair fame gone forever, was valueless to her. She seemed to have but one object in her mind: to find the murderer or murderers of her parents and half-brother. By her

direction the shrewdest of detectives were employed
and money flowed like water, but to no purpose. The
Gordon tragedy remained a mystery. I had consented to
act as one of the trustees of the immense Gordon estates
and business interests, and by my advice the Misses
Gordon went abroad. A year later I received a letter
from Edward Turner, saying that Jeannette Gordon had
died suddenly in Rome, and that Talma, after refusing
all his entreaties for an early marriage, had disappeared,
leaving no clue as to her whereabouts. I could give the
poor fellow no comfort, although I had been duly
notified of the death of Jeannette by Talma, in a letter
telling me where to forward her remittances, and at the
same time requesting me to keep her present residence
secret, especially from Edward.

I had established a sanitarium for the cure of chronic
diseases at Gordonville, and absorbed in the cares of my
profession I gave little thought to the Gordons. I seemed
fated to be involved in mysteries.

A man claiming to be an Englishman, and fresh from
the California gold fields, engaged board and
professional service at my retreat. I found him suffering
in the grasp of tuberculosis — the last stages. He called
himself Simon Cameron. Seldom have I seen so
fascinating and wicked a face. The lines of the mouth
were cruel, the eyes cold and sharp, the smile mocking
and evil. He had money in plenty but seemed to have no
friends, for he had received no letters and had had no
visitors in the time he had been with us. He was an
enigma to me; and his nationality puzzled me, for of

course I did not believe his story of being English. The peaceful influence of the house seemed to soothe him in a measure, and make his last steps to the mysterious valley as easy as possible. For a time he improved, and would sit or walk about the grounds and sing sweet songs for the pleasure of the other inmates. Strange to say, his malady only affected his voice at times. He sang quaint songs in a silvery tenor of great purity and sweetness that was delicious to the listening ear:

> *A wet sheet and a flowing sea*
> *A wind that follows fast*
> *And fills the white and rustling sail*
> *And bends the gallant mast*
> *And bends the gallant mast, my boys*
> *While like the eagle free*
> *Away the good ship flies, and leaves*
> *Old England on the lea.*

There are few singers on the stage who could surpass Simon Cameron.

One night, a few weeks after Cameron's arrival, I sat in my office making up my accounts when the door opened and closed. I glanced up, expecting to see a servant. A lady advanced toward me. She threw back her veil, and then I saw that Talma Gordon, or her ghost, stood before me. After the first excitement of our meeting was over, she told me she had come direct from Paris, to place herself in my care. I had studied her attentively during the first moments of our meeting, and I felt that she was right; unless something unforeseen happened to arouse her from the stupor into which she seemed to have fallen, the last Gordon was doomed to an early death. The next day I told her I had cabled Edward Turner to come to her.

"It will do no good; I cannot marry him," was her only comment.

"Have you no feeling of pity for that faithful fellow?" I asked her sternly, provoked by her seeming indifference. I shall never forget the varied emotions depicted on her speaking face. Fully revealed to my gaze was the sight of a human soul tortured beyond the point of endurance; suffering all things enduring all things, in the silent agony of despair.

In a few days Edward arrived, and Talma consented to see him and explain her refusal to keep her promise to him. "You must be present, Doctor; it is due your long, tried friendship to know that I have not been fickle, but have acted from the best and strongest motives."

I shall never forget that day. It was directly after lunch that we met in the library. I was greatly excited, expecting I knew not what. Edward was agitated, too. Talma was the only calm one. She handed me what seemed to be a letter with the request that I would read it. Even now I think I can repeat every word of the document, so indelibly are the words engraved upon my mind:

My darling sister, Talma,

When you read these lines I shall be no more, for I shall not live to see your life blasted by the same knowledge that has blighted mine.

One evening, about a year before your expected return from Rome, I climbed into a hammock in one corner of the veranda outside the breakfast room windows, intending to spend the twilight hours in lazy comfort, for it was very hot August weather. I fell asleep. I was awakened by voices. Because of the heat the rooms had been left in semi-darkness. As I lay there, lazily enjoying the beauty of the perfect summer night, my wandering thoughts were arrested by words spoken by our father to Mrs. Gordon, for they were the occupants of the breakfast room.

"Never fear, Mary; Johnny shall have it all — money houses, land and business."

"But if you do go first, Jonathan, what will happen if the girls contest the will? People will think that they ought to have the money as it appears to be theirs by law. I never could survive the terrible disgrace of the story."

"Don't borrow trouble; all you would need to do would be to show them papers I have drawn up, and they would be glad to take their annuity and say nothing. After all, I do not think it is so bad. Jeannette can teach, Talma can paint; six hundred dollars a year is quite enough for them."

I had been somewhat mystified by the conversation until now. This last remark solved the riddle. What could he mean? Teach, paint, six hundred a year. With my usual impetuosity I sprang from my resting-place, and in a moment stood in the room confronting my father, and asking what he meant. I could see plainly that both were disconcerted by my unexpected appearance.

"Ah, wretched girl, you have been listening. But what could I expect of your mother's daughter?"

At these words I felt the indignant blood rush to my head in a torrent. So it had been all my life. Before you could remember, Talma, I had felt my little heart swell with anger at the disparaging hints and slurs concerning our mother. Now was my time. I determined that tonight I would know why she was looked upon as an outcast, and her children subjected to every humiliation. So I replied to my father in bitter anger:

"I was not listening; I fell asleep in the hammock. What do you mean by a paltry six hundred a year each to Talma and to me? 'My mother's daughter' demands an explanation from you, sir, of the meaning of the monstrous injustice that you have always practiced toward my sister and me."

"Speak more respectfully to your father, Jeannette," broke in Mrs. Gordon.

"How is it, madam, that you look for respect from one whom you have delighted to torment ever since you came into this most unhappy family?"

"Hush, both of you," said Captain Gordon, who seemed to have recovered from the dismay into which my sudden appearance and passionate words had plunged him. "I think I may as well tell you as to wait. Since you know so much, you may as well know the whole miserable story."

He motioned me to a seat. I could see that he was deeply agitated. I seated myself in a chair he pointed out, in wonder and expectation — expectation of I knew not what. I trembled. This was a supreme moment in my life; I felt it. The air was heavy with the intense stillness that had settled over

us as the common sounds of day gave place to the early quiet
of the rural evening. I could see Mrs. Gordon's face. There
was a smile of triumph upon it. I clinched my hands and bit
my lip until the blood came, in the effort to keep from
screaming What was I about to hear? At last he spoke:

"I was disappointed at your birth, and also at the birth of
Talma. I wanted a male heir. When I knew that I should again
be a father I was torn by hope and fear, but I comforted myself
with the thought that luck would be with me in the birth of
the third child. When the doctor brought me word that a son
was born to the house of Gordon, I was wild with delight, and
did not notice his disturbed countenance. In the midst of my
joy he said to me:

"Captain Gordon, there is something strange about this
birth. I want you to see this child."

Quelling my exultation I followed him to the nursery, and
there, lying in the cradle, I saw a child dark as a mulatto with
the characteristic features of the Negro. I was stunned.
Gradually it dawned upon me that there was something
radically wrong. I turned to the doctor for an explanation.

"There is but one explanation, Captain Gordon; there is
Negro blood in this child."

"There is no Negro blood in my veins," I said proudly.

Then I paused — the mother! — I glanced at the doctor.
He was watching me intently. The same thought was in his
mind. I must have lived a thousand years in that cursed five
seconds that I stood there confronting the physician and
trying to think. "Come," said I to him, "let us end this
suspense." Without thinking of consequences, I hurried away
to your mother and accused her of infidelity to her marriage

vows. I raved like a madman. Your mother fell into convulsions; her life was despaired of. I sent for Mr. and Mrs. Franklin, and then I learned the truth. They were childless. One year while on a Southern tour, they befriended an octoroon girl who had been abandoned by her white lover. Her child was a beautiful girl baby. They, being Northern born, thought little of cast distinction because the child showed no trace of Negro blood They determined to adopt it. They went abroad, secretly sending back word to their friends at a proper time, of the birth of a little daughter. No one doubted the truth of the statement. They made Isabel their heiress, and all went well until the birth of your brother. Your mother and the unfortunate babe died. This is the story which, if known, would bring dire disgrace upon the Gordon family.

To appease my righteous wrath, Mr. Franklin left a codicil to his will by which all the property is left at my disposal. I sat there after he had finished his story, stunned by what I had heard. I understood, now, Mrs. Gordon's half contemptuous toleration and lack of consideration for us both. As I rose from my seat to leave the room I said to Captain Gordon:

"Still, in spite of all, sir, I am a Gordon, legally born. I will not easily give up my birthright."

I left that room a broken-hearted girl, filled with a desire for revenge upon this man, my father, who by his manner disowned us without a regret. Not once in that remarkable interview did he speak of our mother as his wife; he quietly repudiated her and us with all the cold cruelty of relentless caste prejudice. I heard the treatment of your lover's proposal: I knew why Captain Gordon's consent to your marriage was withheld.

The night of the reception and dance was the chance for which I had waited, planned and watched. I crept from my window into the ivy-vines, and so down, down, until I stood upon the window-sill of Captain Gordon's room in the old left tower. How did I do it, you ask? I do not know. The house was silent after the revel; the darkness of the gathering storm favored me, too. The lawyer was there that day. The will was signed and put safely away among my father's papers. I was determined to have the will and the other documents bearing upon the case, and I would have revenge, too, for the cruelties we had suffered. With the old East Indian dagger firmly grasped I entered the room and found that my revenge had been forestalled. The horror of the discovery I made that night restored me to reason and a realisation of the crime I meditated. Scarce knowing what I did, I sought and found the papers, and crept back to my room as I had come. Do you wonder that my disease is past medical aid?

I looked at Edward as I finished. He sat, his face covered with his hands. Finally he looked up with a glance of haggard despair.

"Doctor, but this is too much. I could stand the stigma of murder, but add to that the pollution of Negro blood. No man is brave enough to face such a situation."

"It is as I thought it would be," said Talma sadly, while the tears poured over her white face. "I do not blame you, Edward."

He rose from his chair, wrung my hand in a convulsive clasp, turned to Talma and bowed profoundly, with his eyes fixed upon the floor, hesitated, turned, paused, bowed again and abruptly left the room. So those two who had been lovers, parted. I turned to Talma, expecting her to give way. She smiled a pitiful smile, and said, "You see, Doctor, I knew best."

From that on she failed rapidly. I was restless. If only I could rouse her to an interest in life, she might live to old age. So rich, so young, so beautiful, so talented, so pure; I grew savage thinking of the injustice of the world. I had not reckoned on the power that never sleeps. Something was about to happen.

On visiting Cameron next morning I found him approaching the end. He had been sinking for a week very rapidly. As I sat by the bedside holding his emaciated hand, he fixed his bright, wicked eyes on me, and asked: "How long have I got to live?"

"Candidly, but a few hours."

"Thank you; well, I want death. I am not afraid to die. Doctor, Cameron is not my name."

"I never supposed it was."

"No? You are sharper than I thought. I heard all your talk yesterday with Talma Gordon. Curse the whole race."

He clasped his bony fingers around my arm and gasped, "I murdered the Gordons."

Had I the pen of a Dumas I could not paint Cameron as he told his story. It is a question with me whether this wheeling planet, home of the suffering, doubting, dying, may not hold worse agonies on its smiling surface than those of the conventional hell. I sent for Talma and a lawyer. We gave him stimulants, and then with broken intervals of coughing and prostration we got the story of the Gordon murder I give it to you in a few words:

"I am an East Indian, but my name does not matter, Cameron is as good as any. There is many a soul crying in heaven and hell for vengeance on Jonathan Gordon. Gold was his idol; and many a good man walked the plank, and many a gallant ship was stripped of her treasure, to satisfy his lust for gold. His blackest crime was the murder of my father, who was his friend, and had sailed with him for many a year as mate. One night these two went ashore together to bury their treasure. My father never returned from that expedition. His body was afterward found with a bullet through the heart on the shore where the vessel stopped that night. It was the custom then among pirates for the captain to kill the men who helped bury their treasure. Captain Gordon was no better than a pirate. An East Indian never forgets, and I swore by my mother's deathbed to hunt Captain Gordon down until I had avenged my father's murder. I had the plans of the Gordon estate, and fixed on the night of the reception in honor of Talma as the time for my vengeance. There is a secret entrance from the shore to the chambers where Captain Gordon slept; no one knew of it save the Captain and trusted members of his crew. My mother gave me the plans, and entrance and escape were easy.

"So the great mystery was solved. In a few hours

Cameron was no more. we placed the confession in the hands of the police, and there the matter ended."

"But what became of Talma Gordon?" questioned the president. "Did she die?"

"Gentlemen," said the Doctor, rising to his feet and sweeping the faces of the company with his eagle gaze, "gentlemen, if you will follow me to the drawing room, I shall have much pleasure in introducing you to my wife — née Talma Gordon."

A DASH FOR LIBERTY
Pauline E. Hopkins

"So, Madison, you are bound to try it?"

"Yes, suh," was the respectful reply.

There was silence between the two men for a space, and Mr. Dickson drove his horse to the end of the furrow he was making and returned slowly to the starting point, and the sombre figure awaiting him.

"Do I not pay you enough, and treat you well?" asked the farmer as he halted.

"Yes, suh."

"Then why not stay here and let well enough alone?"

"Liberty is worth nothing to me while my wife is a slave."

"We will manage to get her to you in a year or two."

The man smiled and sadly shook his head. "A year or two would mean forever, situated as we are, Mr. Dickson. It is hard for you to understand; you white men are all alike where you are called upon to judge a

Negro's heart," he continued bitterly. "Imagine yourself in my place; how would you feel? The relentless heel of oppression in the States will have ground my rights as a husband into the dust, and have driven Susan to despair in that time. A white man may take up arms to defend a bit of property; but a black man has no right to his wife, his liberty or his life against his master. This makes me low-spirited, Mr. Dickson, and I have determined to return to Virginia for my wife. My feelings are centred in the idea of liberty," and as he spoke he stretched his arms toward the deep blue of the Canadian sky in a magnificent gesture. Then with a deep-drawn breath that inflated his mighty chest, he repeated the word: "Liberty. I think of it by day and dream of it by night; and I shall only taste it in all its sweetness when Susan shares it with me."

Madison was an unmixed African, of grand physique, and one of the handsomest of his race. His dignified, calm and unaffected bearing marked him as a leader among his fellows. His features bore the stamp of genius. His firm step and piercing eye attracted the attention of all who met him. He had arrived in Canada along with many other fugitives during the year 1840, and being a strong, able-bodied man, and a willing worker, had sought and obtained employment on Mr. Dickson's farm.

After Madison's words, Mr. Dickson stood for some time in meditative silence.

"Madison," he said at length, "there's desperate blood in your veins, and if you get back there and are captured, you'll do desperate deeds."

"Well, put yourself in my place: I shall be there singlehanded. I have a wife whom I love, and whom I will protect. I hate slavery, I hate the laws that make my country a nursery for it. Must I be denied the right of aggressive defense against those who would overpower and crush me by superior force?"

"I understand you fully, Madison; it is not your defense but your rashness that I fear. Promise me that you will be discreet, and not begin an attack." Madison hesitated. Such a promise seemed to him like surrendering a part of those individual rights for which he panted. Mr. Dickson waited. Presently the Negro said significantly: "I promise not to be indiscreet."

There were tears in the eyes of the kind-hearted farmer as he pressed Madison's hand.

"God speed and keep you and the wife you love; may she prove worthy."

In a few days Madison received the wages due him, and armed with tiny saws and files to cut a way to liberty, if captured, turned his face toward the South.

It was late in the fall of 1840 when Madison found himself again at home in the fair Virginia State. The land was blossoming into ripe maturity, and the smiling fields lay waiting for the harvester.

The fugitive, unable to travel in the open day, had hidden himself for three weeks in the shadow of the friendly forest near his old home, filled with hope and fear, unable to obtain any information about the wife he hoped to rescue from slavery. After weary days and nights, he had reached the most perilous part of his mission. Tonight there would be no moon and the clouds threatened a storm; to his listening ears the rising wind bore the sound of laughter and singing. He drew back into the deepest shadow. The words came distinctly to his ears as the singers neared his hiding place.

> *All them pretty gals will be there,*
> *Shuck that corn before you eat.*
> *They will fix it for us rare,*
> *Shuck that corn before you eat.*
> *I know that supper will be big,*
> *Shuck that corn before you eat.*
> *I think I smell a fine roast pig,*
> *Shuck that corn before you eat.*
> *Stuff that coon and bake him down,*
> *I spec some niggers there from town.*
> *Shuck that corn before you eat.*
> *Please cook that turkey nice and brown.*
> *By the side of that turkey I'll be found,*
> *Shuck that corn before you eat.*

"Don't talk about that turkey; he'll be gone before we get there."

"He's talking, ain't he?"

"Last time I shucked corn, turkey was the toughest meat I ate for many a day; you've got to have teeth sharp like a saw to eat it."

"S'pose you ain't got no teeth, then what you going to do?"

"Why, if you ain't got no teeth you must gum it."

"Ha, ha, ha."

Madison glided in and out among the trees, listening until he was sure that it was a gang going to a corn-shucking, and he resolved to join it, and get, if possible some news of Susan. He came out upon the highway, and as the company reached his hiding place, he fell into the ranks and joined in the singing. The darkness hid his identity from the company while he learned from their conversation the important events of the day.

On they marched by the light of weird, flaring pine knots, singing their merry cadences, in which the noble minor strains habitual to Negro music, sounded the depths of sadness, glancing off in majestic harmony, that touched the very gates of paradise in suppliant prayer.

It was close to midnight; the stars had disappeared and a steady rain was falling when, by a circuitous route, Madison reached the mansion where he had learned that his wife was still living. There were lights in the windows. Mirth at the great house kept company with mirth at the quarters.

The fugitive stole noiselessly under the fragrant magnolia trees and paused, asking himself what he should do next. As he stood there he heard the hoof-beats of the mounted patrol far in the distance, die into silence. Cautiously he drew near the house and crept around to the rear of the building directly beneath the window of his wife's sleeping closet. He swung himself up and tried it; it yielded to his touch. Softly he raised the sash, and softly he crept into the room. His foot struck against an object and swept it to the floor. It fell with a loud crash. In an instant the door opened. There was a rush of feet, and Madison stood at bay. The house was aroused; lights were brought.

"I knowed it was him," cried the overseer in triumph. "I heard him a-getting in the window, but I kept dark 'til he knocked my gun down; then I grabbed him. I knowed this room'd trap him if we was patient about it."

Madison shook his captor off and backed against the wall. His grasp tightened on the club in his hand, his nerves were like steel, his eyes flashed fire.

"Don't kill him," shouted Judge Johnson, as the overseer's pistol gleamed in the light. "Five hundred dollars for him alive."

With a crash, Madison's club descended on the head of the nearest man; again, and yet again, he whirled it around, doing frightful execution each time it fell. Three of the men who had responded to the overseer's cry for help were on the ground, and he himself was sore from many wounds before weakened by loss of blood, Madison finally succumbed.

The brig *Creole* lay at the Richmond dock taking on her cargo of tobacco, hemp, flax and slaves. The sky was cloudless, and the blue waters rippled but slightly under the faint breeze. There was on board the confusion incident to departure. In the hold and on deck men were hurrying to and fro, busy and excited, making the final preparations for the voyage. The slaves came aboard in two gangs: first the men, chained like cattle, were marched to their quarters in the hold; then came the women to whom more freedom was allowed.

In spite of the blue sky and the bright sunlight that silvered the water, the scene was indescribably depressing and sad. The procession of gloomy-faced men and weeping women seemed to be descending into a living grave.

The captain and the first mate were standing together at the head of the gangway as the women stepped aboard. Most were very plain and bore the marks of servitude, a few were neat and attractive in appearance; but one was a woman whose great beauty immediately attracted attention. She was an octoroon. It was a tradition that her grandfather had served in the Revolutionary War, as well as in both Houses of Congress. That was nothing, however, at a time when the blood of the proudest F. F. V.'s was freely mingled with that of the African slaves on their plantations. Who wonders that Virginia has produced great men of color from among the ex-bondmen, or, that illustrious black men proudly point to Virginia as a birthplace? Posterity rises to the plane that their ancestors bequeath, and the most refined, the wealthiest and the most intellectual whites of that proud State have not hesitated to amalgamate with the Negro.

"What a beauty," exclaimed the captain as the line of women paused a moment opposite him.

"Yes," said the overseer in charge of the gang. "She's as fine a piece of flesh as I have had in trade for many a day."

"What's the price?" demanded the captain.

"Oh, way up. Two or three thousand. She's a lady's maid, well-educated, and can sing and dance. We'll get it in New Orleans. Like to buy?"

"You don't suit my pile," was the reply, as his eyes followed the retreating form of the handsome octoroon. "Give her a cabin to herself; she ought not to herd with the rest," he continued, turning to the mate.

He turned with a meaning laugh to execute the order.

The *Creole* proceeded slowly on her way towards New Orleans. In the men's cabin, Madison Monroe lay chained to the floor and heavily ironed. But from the first moment on board ship he had been busily engaged in selecting men who could be trusted in the dash for liberty that he was determined to make. The miniature files and saws which he still wore concealed in his clothing were faithfully used in the darkness of night. The man was at peace, although he had caught no glimpse of the dearly loved Susan. When the body suffers greatly, the strain upon the heart becomes less tense, and a welcome calmness had stolen over the prisoner's soul.

On the ninth day out the brig encountered a rough sea, and most of the slaves were sick, and therefore not watched with very great vigilance. This was the time for action, and it was planned that they should rise that night. Night came on; the first watch was summoned; the wind was blowing high. Along the narrow passageway that separated the men's quarters from the women's, a man was creeping.

The octoroon lay upon the floor of her cabin, apparently sleeping, when a shadow darkened the door, and the captain stepped into the room, casting bold glances at the reclining figure. Profound silence reigned. One might have fancied one self on a deserted vessel, but for the sound of an occasional footstep on the deck above, and the murmur of voices in the opposite hold.

She lay stretched at full length with her head resting upon her arm, a position that displayed to the best advantage the perfect symmetry of her superb figure; the dim light of a lantern played upon the long black ringlets, finely-chiselled mouth and well-rounded chin, upon the marbled skin veined by her master's blood — representative of two races, to which did she belong?

For a moment the man gazed at her in silence; then casting a glance around him, he dropped upon one knee and kissed the sleeping woman full upon the mouth.

With a shriek the startled sleeper sprang to her feet. The woman's heart stood still with horror; she recognised the intruder as she dashed his face aside with both hands.

"None of that, my beauty," growled the man, as he reeled back with an oath, and then flung himself forward and threw his arm about her slender waist.

"Why did you think you had a private cabin, and all the delicacies of the season? Not to behave like a young catamount, I warrant you."

The passion of terror and desperation lent the girl such strength that the man was forced to relax his hold slightly. Quick as a flash, she struck him a stinging blow across the eyes, and as he staggered back, she sprang out of the doorway, making for the deck with the evident intention of going overboard.

"God have mercy," broke from her lips as she passed the men's cabin, closely followed by the captain.

"Hold on, girl; we'll protect you," shouted Madison, and he stooped, seized the heavy padlock which fastened the iron ring that encircled his ankle to the iron bar, and stiffening the muscles, wrenched the fastening apart, and hurled it with all his force straight at the captain's head.

His aim was correct. The padlock hit the captain not far from the left temple. The blow stunned him. In a moment Madison was upon him and had seized his weapons, another moment served to handcuff the unconscious man.

"If the fire of Heaven were in my hands, I would throw it at these cowardly whites. Follow me: it is liberty or death," he shouted as he rushed for the quarter-deck. Eighteen others followed him, all of whom seized whatever they could wield as weapons.

The crew were all on deck; the three passengers were seated on the companion smoking. The appearance of the slaves all at once completely surprised the whites.

So swift were Madison's movements that at first the officers made no attempt to use their weapons; but this was only for an instant. One of the passengers drew his pistol, fired, and killed one of the blacks. The next moment he lay dead upon the deck from a blow with a piece of a capstan bar in Madison's hand. The fight then became general, passengers and crew taking part.

The first and second mates were stretched out upon the deck with a single blow each. The sailors ran up the rigging for safety, and in short time Madison was master of the *Creole*.

After his accomplices had covered the slaver's deck, the intrepid leader forbade the shedding of more blood. The sailors came down to the deck, and their wounds were dressed. All the prisoners were heavily ironed and well guarded except the mate, who was to navigate the vessel; with a musket doubly charged pointed at his breast, he was made to swear to take the brig into a British port.

By one splendid and heroic stroke, the daring Madison had not only gained his own liberty, but that of one hundred and thirty-four others.

The next morning all the slaves who were still fettered, were released, and the cook was ordered to prepare the best breakfast that the stores would permit; this was to be a fete in honor of the success of the revolt and as a surprise to the females whom the men had not yet seen.

As the women filed into the captain's cabin, where the meal was served, weeping, singing and shouting over their deliverance, the beautiful octoroon with one wild, half-frantic cry of joy sprang towards the gallant leader.

"Madison."

"My God, Susan. My wife."

She was locked to his breast; she clung to him convulsively. Unnerved at last by the revulsion to more than relief and ecstacy, she broke into wild sobs, while the astonished company closed around them with loud hurrahs.

Madison's cup of joy was filled to the brim. He clasped her to him in silence, and humbly thanked Heaven for its blessing and mercy.

The next morning the *Creole* landed at Nassau, New Providence, where the slaves were offered protection and hospitality.

Every act of oppression is a weapon for the oppressed. Right is a dangerous instrument; woe to us if our enemy wields it.

END